MAERDYM

BOOK ONE: SAVER

By

DARNELL R. TUCKER

Contents

Maerdym

BOOK ONE: SAVER

The Time Before

It all began with a dream. God, Evolution, or mere coincidence. Whatever one's preference, the birth of life, started with the motivation to live...

We were never alone. From the very beginning Earthlings existed only to dream, and dreams lived only by being dreamt. An intricate concept that has eluded the mental grasp of the most gifted scientists. What experiments must be run, what theories must be tested to understand the true meaning of a dream? Or were they ever meant to be understood at all?

Maerdym is home to every stretch of fantasy. One's biggest fears and one's greatest desires, it's the world that holds no boundaries to imagination and restricts nothing from sanity. Maerdym is where all dreams go, but every dream must come to an end right? Not exactly...

Powerful thunder rang through the night sky accompanied by a downpour that seemed never ending. Voices of excitement filled the air, but they were only heard on the opposite half of the city. This half was dead silent. A boy's hard footsteps sound like boulders as his boots pound on the puddles of rain water beneath him. The sound of this continuous battering is balanced out by the boy's deep breaths. The brown in his hair is more defined while wet and the rain on his glasses make it difficult for him to navigate. The many tears in his clothes reveal an exhausted body, but this body cannot stop running, because this boy is running for his life!

"Why don't you stop running Super?!" a voice yells from behind. "You are my best friend so I promise to kill you quickly!"

Super is pursued by another small boy with much different features, long black hair, ghostly pale skin, and a couple of hatred-stained knives in his hands. For miles the boys run through the dark half of the city. Super cuts down a pitch black alley hoping to lose his hunter in the shadows. Sweat, along with fear, runs down Super's face as the alley begins to narrow. His marathon comes to an end when he finds himself face to face with a brick wall and nowhere else to run. With no other options he turns to face the long haired boy.

"Genie why are you doing this?!" Super screams. His voice emits a perfect blend of fear and desperation. His words make Genie stop and lower his knives.

"Why do you keep calling me that? We have been best friends our entire lives and you still haven't given me a name!"

"You're right we HAVE been best friends our entire lives! We don't need names for everybody else to call us; we have our names for each other! Just like we never needed parents and we never needed siblings! We're different than everybody else and you know that! I call you Genie because you can make anything you want come true! I don't know how we can make our dreams come to life but you're way better at it than me. That's why we left the orphanage remember? Do you remember why you call me Super?"

Genie tried to recall the reason behind Super's nickname. Then he raised his head to meet Super's eyes. "It's because you always try to save everything. It doesn't matter what it is, a bug, a cat, anything! You could never stand and watch, you had to help it.

"Yeah see there you go!" Super exclaimed in excitement. He felt his words somehow getting through to his former friend.

"But this is exactly why I have to kill you Super!"

Super's expression dropped like the freefalling rain around him. This conclusion made no sense to him.

"Last night, I had another dream. I dreamt of... ruling the world!"

Super flinched backward in shock.

"With my power I could do it! Like you said we are both different but my abilities are better than yours! I can have anything I want! Whatever I dream will come true! In my dream though, there was one person stopping me, YOU! You just couldn't accept me and you stopped me from having whatever I wanted. I won't let that dream come true!"

"Genie, what's the matter with you? Why do you want everything? Why can't you just be happy with what you have?!"

Super's words no longer show any effect on Genie. Genie's dark brown eyes begin to stare into the distance. His attention is focused elsewhere. Almost like-

"-He's daydreaming! I can make my dreams real, but Genie can make his daydreams real! That's why he can have whatever he wants!"

Super hurries toward his friend but he is too slow. Bright glowing portals surround him like a swarm of bees around a stingy bear. A group of knives identical to the ones in Genie's hands fly out of the portals and close in on Super, but without hesitation he protects himself with a barrier of black holes that swallow the blades.

"You always used to wake up in cold sweats because of your black hole dreams," said Genie in anger. "Back then it irritated me, but now it's just plain pissing me off!"

"Stop this Genie! We can work this out!"

Again Super was ignored. He slips into his daze once more, signifying a daydream being formed.

"This is it Super. Our dreams clash so I have to kill you in order to keep my dream alive!"

"Genie, NO!-" Super's cry fades into a distorted screech. His body begins to shrink. His arms and legs wither into their sleeves and his head follows along. Genie is slowly shrunk to nothing but a pile of clothes and a baby's cry. Genie creeps toward the stack of clothing and pulls back the ripped green shirt revealing Super but now as a newborn.

"This way you won't be able to resist anymore. So, I am all powerful!" Genie says to himself with a collection of malice in his eyes. "Goodbye, best friend."

Genie holds the knives cross bladed to the infant's neck. His fond memories cause his body to pause, but the hatred in his heart strengthens his grip on the blades. The steel is so sharply tight at the baby's throat that a small drop of blood runs down its neck. In a synchronized uproar the rain, thunder, and baby's cry intensify. Genie at last prepares to end Super's life. His forearms tighten and his nostrils flare, NOW!"

From the concrete beneath his feet opens yet another dimensional gate but this one is much larger. It surrounds the area he's standing on and then some. From the new portal emerges first the nose, then the head of a massive great white. The king of the sea rises straight over Genie. He isn't given a second to react because in no time his body is engulfed by the sharks gargantuan jaw set. Without as much as a scream the boy is swallowed whole by the aquatic demon, who then returns to the vanishing portal.

The rooftops are now flooded, but water isn't the only substance lurking in the shadows.

"Why did you kill him? He wasn't the sacrifice," a voice speaks. Under the moon's dark shine stands a being almost completely covered in clothing. His face is shrouded by a dark mask and no skin is barred from his neck down. Only partial images of his blood shot eyes can be seen through his long black hair.

"We can't have the Saver Piece die at this time. His role in the future events will be too crucial to leave to chance," a second voice responds. This figure is much neater looking. His skin is light brown and hair cut low with a fine edge. He is tall and stands with a powerful presence as his trench coat blows in the wind. "Chosen, you and I stand witness to the future's only chance of survival. If he dies now, it may be a hundred years before the Saver Piece is reincarnated. At least this way he may be mature enough when the time comes for planet Earth to ask for his help."

"Why do you care?" Chosen asks. "You have never cared about anything or anyone Callous."

"If mankind dies, I die with it. It's as simple as that. Sometimes life requires us to make sacrifices in order to help the greater cause, but you know that more than anyone else, don't you?"

Chosen shuts his eyes as he speaks. "A sacrifice is but another piece of the puzzle. I am ready to fulfill my duty."

Without another word Callous rams a long blade through Chosen's heart. The boy first drops to his knees, then face first into the puddle beneath him. In a simultaneous action the rain stops and the thunder silences.

"You are right, there must be a sacrifice. Perhaps the day will come when man understands why, but for now all we can do is accept Maerdym's shackles and continue being slaves to our own dreams.

The Time Before part 2: Professor Save

Many years have passed since that incident. The year is 2035. Planet Earth had seen peace for a while. It allowed many nations to lower their guard and grow accustomed to this lax way of life. But in the darkest corners of the earth, an evil was manifesting. It was an evil that grew with the dark thoughts of mankind. Its very existence proved that even when times are favorable, there is always hatred lurking in the heart of humanity.

But there was one man who knew of this evil. He was a professor at the University of Southern California. There he went by the name of Professor Save, though his true identity was different in every record kept of him. He held no real defining characteristics. He was average size, about 5'11, 175 pounds. He had a typical middle aged Caucasian male look with thick glasses, nothing out of the ordinary. But despite his appearance, this man was all but ordinary. He took great pride in his position at USC. The class he taught was...

"Introduction to Maerdym studies. Everyone welcome, to introduction to maerdym studies." Save announced to his spring semester class. "I am your instructor, Professor Save. If you want, you can call me Save, or any other clever nickname you come up with, Ha-ha."

As the students got comfortable in their seat, the restless noises began to die down. But with it came the uneasy chatter of confusion.

"Um how about we get your full name?" A young lady shouts out from the back of the class. But it seemed to get more of a response from the students than the teacher.

"Now, moving right along." Save continues as though he didn't hear the comment. You class, have just embarked on your first day, of enlightenment.

Save begins to sway between all sides of the class as though he were preaching to a church of college students.

"Now hear me out. What if I were to tell you that everything you've ever dreamed, your biggest fears, your greatest desires, even your wildest fantasies are all real. And what if everything you thought you knew about reality was completely wrong, but at the same time entirely true? Now before we get any further let me start by saying mastering maerdym is no easy task-"

"-Wait a minute hold up!" An outspoken freshmen in the center of the classroom rises to his feet in an uproar. He catches the eyes of every person in the room. "So you mean to tell me that what everybody says about you is really true?"

"Well sir I'm not exactly sure what everyone says. Please enlighten me."

"Well basically rumors are that you're a crazy ass loser who believes in fairy tales." The room overflows with laughter.

"I really had to see it for myself. But I gotta bounce or I'm gonna be late for football practice."

He snaps his finger as he heads out the door with eighty percent of the class behind him. Save stands at the front of the class in an awkward pause. The room is now withered down to a handful of students. But even they begin to pack their folders and zip their backpacks.

"I'm sorry mister uh Save, but I wasn't exactly sure what this class entailed. I joined out of curiosity."

"Same here sir"

"Yes me as well."

Save smiles at the remaining students.

"It's fine guys I understand. I wish you all the most of luck in your college careers."

The remainder of the class leaves the room, all but one. Sitting in the very front of the class is a skinny little boy with red hair. His clothes are wrinkled and his wrists are covered with a gallery of different watches. He sits patiently as though waiting to begin taking notes.

"Um excuse me young man," Save addresses him. "But aren't you going to leave with the rest of the class?"

"Oh heavens no sir! I have been waiting my entire high school career to be able to take this class. Every since I began researching the University of Southern California and stumbled across a professor with such a strong belief in this dream world called Maerdym. I couldn't ignore it sir. I too share your beliefs and despite what people say I don't think you are a loser."

"Ha-ha well it's nice to know that someone still holds an open mind around here. Also it's reassuring that not everyone can be so easily persuaded by the football team's star running back."

"Ha-ha everyone answers to time sir. In a few years that star running back will more than likely be doing maintenance on my automated grocery bagger."

The two share a laugh.

"Oh by the way sir my name is Glen Heard."

"Well it's nice to meet you Glen. And I promise that as long as I have at least one student, I'll be here every day to teach."

"And I'll be here every day to learn sir."

After class, the two walk together outside on University campus. They hear the buzz of the new fast-tran shuttles being used by students trying to get to their next class in a hurry. There is also a hologram screen above the administration buildings giving information on some of the upcoming events being held.

"I see you finally found someone who will actually listen to you this time, huh Professor?"

A voice from someone behind is heard. The two turn around and Glen is stunned to see that voice is accompanied by a beautiful figure. Her long dark hair and gorgeous eyes makes Glen think that she has them mistaken for someone else, this Spanish goddess couldn't be conversing with a couple of nerds?

"Hi there, I'm Sarah Rector. And you are?"

Sarah extends her hand to Glen, but the gesture isn't returned. Glen's hands begin to sweat and his face turns redder than his hair.

"Don't be shy Glen. This is my good friend Sarah."

"Shy huh?" Sarah exclaims. "Oh thank goodness! For a second there I thought it was my new perfume."

Sarah's humor breaks the ice and makes Glen feel more comfortable. He, Sarah, and Save go to the cafeteria for lunch.

"So Mrs. Rector, I don't remember seeing your name on any of the enrollment forms." Glen says while still wiping his hands on his shirt. Are you a professor here also?

Sarah clears her throat.

"It's actually *Ms.* Rector, Glen. Your teacher hasn't popped the question yet ha-ha." She glances at Save who is now blushing and fixing his glasses. Sarah looks back at Glen. And as for being a professor, the answer is no. I'm a faculty counselor here. I'm also the voice keeping Save here to teach his Maerdym studies. If only people would hear him out though, I wouldn't have to defend his position at every conference meeting. Sarah looks at Save again, only this time with a deeper stare. Save sighs in disappointment.

"So does that mean you believe in Maerdym too?" Glen asks, interrupting their gaze.

"Oh of course, I find it inspiring that such a world exists, a world where all dreams come true. Anyone can be anything. Your only boundaries are your own minds limitations. I believe that we can put an end to any chance of war and sorrow by knowing how to access Maerdym."

"Oh I think the same!" Glens stands from his seat. Consider we used Maerdym to travel in time. We could rewrite history; fix all the mistakes we've made in the past. We could even move forward! Prevent the mistakes in the future."

"That's an intriguing thought Glen but not what I had in mind. Instead of tampering with time, why not make time irrelevant? Old age, diseases, lingering injuries, they can all be nullified with Maerdym. Immortality is the key. If no one dies, than no one will have a reason to kill."

"Ha-ha and I thought I was the nerd." Save thinks to himself. These two give the word a whole new meaning.

Just then sirens go off throughout the room! There is an outstanding increase in chatter but it is drowned out by the intercom speakers. Soon a voice starts delivering a message.

"Attention all students and faculty, please tune in to your Global Communicators immediately! We are under a state of emergency!"

The University campus is thrown in frenzy. Hearts are pounding, while the tension grows by the second. People reach in their pockets for their Global Communicators.

"Save what's going on?" Sarah asks in a frantic confusion.

Professor Save gives no response. He goes into his coat pocket to see what the emergency is. But no one is prepared for what they witness.

"…Yes if you are just tuning in, you are watching live footage of the skies over Japan. What you see is indeed what it looks like viewers. About thirteen minutes ago, sixty five missiles were simultaneously launched from countries around the world. But that isn't the worst of the news. These missiles have been run through the government's data trackers and their crash course is set for no other than, the U.S. Ladies and gentlemen, America is under attack! Government officials are speaking with neighboring countries to resolve this conflict and hopefully redirect the missiles somewhere less harmful. But according to reports, the stories are all the same. Countries say they have no explanation for the launches and that their control over their flight path is nonexistent. Coincidently, though all coming from different directions, every projectile is set for impact in one hour…"

"Save I'm scared! Does this mean we all have sixty minutes to live?" Sarah shouts.

"NO! Thi... This can't be real! It must be a dream!" Glen falls to his knees while pulling his hair. Wait... dream! That's it! Professor you can stop this!

"No. No Glen this. This is out of my hands. I've studied Maerdym my whole life but I've yet to use it."

There is a pause between the three. The mayhem around them makes their moment of calm look like they are in their own dimension in a sea of chaos. They stare at each other. Neither one can believe what is happening. Maerdym, if there were such a world, would they ever see it?

Chapter 1: Assassin

The room is dark. There are a few dim lights around but their shine barely makes ones hands visible. Darrel lifts his head which is shrouded in a black hood. His eyes emit an evergreen glow that pierces through the shadows, though his dark skin creates a perfect camouflage, concealing his presence. He diligently scans the room.

"One, two, he's got three body guards." Darrel counts in his head. "Maybe they will make this job more interesting. And the big fat guy at the table must be Perro Gonzales. My target, he fits the description I got, an overgrown slob in nice clothes."

Darrel reaches to his side as to pull out a weapon. His hands stops and he senses a slight hesitation in his movement.

"No. I have to do this. I have no choice. It's for Manny... Damn! Why do I do this every time? Just do it. DO IT!"

Darrel's inner struggle forces him to reject his morals. He resumes reaching to his side. His hand sank into a glow with a luxurious flare, burning with a heat fueled by lost imagination. When it fades an exquisitely designed dagger appears in his hand. The pattern on the handle is green and gold, and there is a wolf symbol flowing onto the blade. Darrel stares deeply into the dagger.

"I don't fully understand Maerdym yet. But as long as I can use it to access my dreams I don't care much about the details. There aren't many like me. But I wonder... I wonder if my father would be proud. I know he also killed for a living. Well, it doesn't matter. We all gotta eat."

Darrel is a hired assassin. He lives with his brother and the only way to survive is to take the lives of others for bounty. His duties have led him here to kill a man he knows nothing about but his name, Perro Gonzales.

Darrel is also a Chaser, meaning he is able to open temporary gates to the dream world known as Maerdym. Using Maerdym allows him to pull dreams from there and materialize them in the real world.

"Now, how am I going to go about doing this?" Darrel's eyes again wander the room. "Of the three guards the one closest to me easily has the thinnest body type. He probably has the quickest reflexes too. That means I need to take him out first."

Darrel then starts to feel a tingling feeling behind his nose. His mouth opens and the feeling begins to build.

"No I can't sneeze now!"

But it builds more and more until he can't hold it in anymore. It reaches its peak!

"Hold it in Darrel!" He commands himself. "Hold it!"

Finally a loud sneeze is released.

"AACHUU!"

Darrel presses his palm against his nose to contain himself. He resisted the urge.

"He sneezed, the closest guard. This is my chance!" Darrel processes the situation in a split second. "NOW!"

Without a moment's notice his body tenses up. His calves tighten to prepare for a leap. His heart pounds against his chest. His grip on the dagger in his right hand amplifies till it seems like he's going to snap it in half. Everything's ready.

"DO IT!"

But wait! Darrel's entire body pauses with the abruptness of a locomotive hitting a steel wall. His breathes are hard. His focus is now on the new body in the room. A woman has entered through the door.

"Bless you." She speaks.

A woman? No a girl. No older than fifteen at the most.

"Eh thanks." The guard responds.

The girl walks forward and stops in the center of the room. Her clothes are ragged and torn. Her hair is long and tangled. Her fear is as clear as day. She can't hide it. Perro looks up at her and grins.

"Ah, little Tania," Perro says with a deceptive smile. The rolls under his chin wrinkle up in a disgusting way. His smile reveals a set of teeth covered in gold caps. "What brings you here today my girl?"

Tania looks down, she can't bear to look him in the eyes. She closes her eyes as she starts to speak.

"You prmm," she stuttered.

"I what?"

"You promised," she whispers.

"Speak Girl!"

"Perro, you promised you would leave us alone. You said my family would be safe. I... I did what you told me to."

As the girl's voice grew so did Perro's level of amusement.

"Oh did you? Well maybe I've gone and forgotten what you did. Ha-ha maybe I need a little reminder," said Perro with an ugly smirk. He then looks around the room at his guards. "What do you think boys?"

The room fills with laughter between Perro and his guards.

"Oh yeah!"

"That's right boss!"

"AACHUU!"

"Bl... bless you." Tania fights her hardest but her efforts aren't enough to hold back her tears.

Tania's body begins to tremble. She crosses her arms and stands tight to her position as though standing in the cold.

"What's the matter, girl?" Perro questions. "Surely you can't still be shy, ha-ha-ha."

"My brother." Tania begins to shake like a volcano fighting back the urge to explode, but the resistance of a young girl is only so strong. Tears begin streaming down her face. "They killed my brother! I did what you said and they killed him anyway! You said you would keep your thugs away from us. But now he's dead! And..." Tania pauses as though just coming to a realization. "He's never coming back." Her strength fades as she falls to her knees.

The laughter from Perro and his men starts to die down.

"Well Girl?"

Tania halts her crying. Her arms slowly drop to her side. She gathers her bravery and rejects her pride. As though breaking from a frozen prison she tries to rise to her feet.

But midway to the top she notices something, a dark red liquid on the ground. There is blood covering the floor. Tania lets out a high pitch scream!

She jumps back away from the blood and starts examining herself.

"Am I bleeding?" She thinks.

No matter how hard she searches she can't find the source of the blood.

"No, it's not from me, then who?

Just then there is a loud thud. A body falls to the ground. One of the bodyguards is dead, the thinnest guard. The other two guards start to shout!

"What the hell happ... AGH!"

Tania screams again as another guard falls to the ground with blood jetting from his neck!

The final guard stands in horror at the sight of his dead comrades. He quickly reaches for his firearms, but it's too late. The second he touches his pistol, his movement stops and he gasps as though choking on the bones of the afterlife. First he drops to his knees clenching his throat, and then flops on his chest to his demise.

"You treacherous girl what have you done?!"

Even Perro realizes she couldn't have done this. His statement receives no response from the trembling Tania who is now curled in a ball on the floor.

The room pauses with a dead silence. A deep omnificence voice brings life back to the room.

"You fat sick bastard." Darrel makes his presence known in the middle of the floor.

A light hanging from the ceiling has begun swinging, seemingly from Darrel's movements around the room. The light it casts fades Darrel's face in and out. His hood is off, revealing his short curly dark brown hair. Under his blood stained jacket is a crimson vest that reflects the light.

"It's been a while since I've been to San Diego. I never would have guessed it would end up this corrupt."

Darrel's voice filled the room.

"Who the hell are you? And how did you kill those three without even being noticed?"

"Humph. Well I was here to kill you for a quick buck. You were a mission and nothing else to me, but now... You've given me a personal motivation.

Everything about you makes me sick, Perro. You don't deserve to live. So my duty to kill you is a lot more enjoyable now."

"Ha-ha-ha-ha! You? Kill me? Do you know who I am? I run the streets of San Diego now. This is my town!

Darrel turns his back to Perro as if he didn't hear a word he said. He stares at Tania who is now gazing in disbelief at her savior. He slowly walks toward her. Her eyes open wider and wider. He kneels down to her but she pulls away in fear. Perro can't believe the situation. Darrel tries to comfort Tania.

"Don't worry. He's never gonna hurt you again. I'm going to end this. Now I want you to pack your things and get you and your family out of this town."

Tania wipes her face as she tries to talk. "But, we have nowhere to go."

"Head to Corona. If you go northeast of here you should get there in a couple of hours."

She takes a second to think about all that's happening. Tania then accepts this blessing and responds. "I... I will. Thank you."

Darrel ascends to a standing position. He turns his body to face Perro again. He then drops his eyes to the floor as he speaks to Tania once more.

"Tania right? Tania I'm sorry about your brother. I have a brother of my own and I'd go crazy if anything ever happened to him. Just know that he's in a better place now. But you should get out of here now."

Tania stands up. She takes a deep breath and closes her eyes.

"No."

"What?"

"I... I... I want to see him die, with my own eyes."

Darrel thinks to himself before answering.

"Fine."

"Ha-ha-ha-ha-ha! You simpletons make me laugh. Do you know who you're messing wi-"

"-Look around you dumbass! There's no one left to protect you. You're all alone Perro!"

Perro looks around the now empty room. One-by-one he looks at his dead body guards. The realization of being alone has now dawned on the corrupt tyrant like a terminal patient who knows he's not going to make it.

"Someone help me!" Perro screams as he waddles to his feet. He dashes for the exit while wheezing and gasping for air. His attempt to escape is pathetic and hard to watch for Darrel.

"Let's end this!" Darrel shouts.

Crash! Perro's back is pressed against the cracked wall, with Darrel's dagger in his chest! Darrel feels Perro's soul instantly slip into the next life.

"He's dead," Darrel says while letting Perro's body drop to the floor.

Tania feels the relief of her life's burden lifted.

"Thank you so much. Can I ask you what your name is?"

Darrel turned to Tania.

"The name's Darrel. I know you must think I'm a good guy but, I'm not. I do this for a living. I'm not proud of it."

"But what about your brother?"

"What about him?"

"Does he approve of this?"

"He's a kid. He wouldn't understand so I don't find any point in telling him. But everything I do, good or bad, is for him. I'm all he's got."

"Then, in a way it's okay. You provide for your brother and take bad people out of this world. You're the saver in my eyes."

"Don't you mean savior?"

Tania smiled and said nothing.

Darrel disregards her statement and continues to get her away from the bloody room they occupied. "Anyways you get out of here. Maybe I'll see you around. I live near Corona myself. If not, good luck with the rest of your life. It should be a lot easier now."

"Thank you for everything Darrel. I'll never forget you."

Chapter 2: Darrel and Manny

Darrel slowly walked up to the entrance of his run-down apartments. He stopped at the password machine and dropped his tool bag on the ground. Darrel closed his eyes and inhaled a deep breath of the sweet spring air. When he reopened them he surveyed his surroundings. His apartment complex stood tall but many of the apartments were vacant. Dried-up leaves blanketed the ground and the sidewalks were plagued with cracks and empty soda cans. Outside of the apartments is nothing but deserted hills as far as the eye can see. At one point of the year these hills were mainly dirt and rocks, though were now covered with green grass due to the rainy winter.

Darrel entered the code to open the gate. After picking his bag back up, he strolled down the sidewalk admiring the flower pedals blowing past him.

"I hope every day of spring this year is like this one," he thought to himself.

Winding around the wash house he noticed an unusual amount of people standing outside in the parking spaces.

"I wonder what happened. The cops are here too. Damn I hope this has nothing to do with me."

Darrel stopped and looked around.

"Wait. Where's Manny?"

Darrel's stride quickened. It soon became a sprint as he threw his bag to the ground once more and searched for his little brother.

"Manny! Manny!" he called. "Hey has anyone seen Manny?"

People's attention slowly turned to the now frantic big brother. Darrel spotted out a police officer and began questioning him.

"Officer, what happened? Well, never mind that. Where's my little brother?"

"Calm down son!" the police officer answered with a confused look on his face.

"Doggie," a light voice said out of nowhere.

Darrel turned to his left. Relief struck as he saw Manny standing in the crowd. A small boy with curly hair that was a bit longer than his older brother. He wore a baggy long sleeved shirt with a pair of baggy jeans. His boyish face lit up when he saw his brother.

"Monkey! Whew! Thought I lost you for second there little bro," he said while rubbing Manny's head.

"Nope. How was work Doggie?"

"Oh uh."

Darrel looked down and noticed he left his tool bag down the street.

"C'mon lets go get my bag real quick."

"Okay. Did you get shocked today?"

"Ha-ha, no not today Monkey," Darrel replied as the two began walking down the street. "So what's going on here? What happened?"

"I guess somebody broke into one of the apartments or somethin."

"You're kidding?"

"Nope, Mr. Peng was really mad. He went off on everybody, even the cops."

"So it was Mr. Peng's apartment? He didn't say anything to you did he?" Darrel asked as he picked up his tool bag.

"Well, no but…"

"Ah so the criminal returns to the scene of the crime!" says an irritating tone.

"What do you mean Mr. Peng?" Darrel asks.

Mr. Peng, a very stern looking man with tightly buttoned clothes.

"Don't act dumb with me boy! I've always been suspicious of you two. We never had a break in until now. Coincidently you hoockos moved in only two months ago! I knew it was you the moment I came home to see my apartment broken into!"

Mr. Peng's commotion began drawing its own crowd from the one earlier. His wife soon rushes over and grabs him.

"Jerald that's enough! Leave these boys alone!" she screams.

"Boys is right! Look at you. You are a kid yourself. What are you doing raising another kid? How old are you anyway boy?"

Mr. Peng's question raises the eyebrows of the police officers who are now making their way to the new crowd.

"Eighteen sir," Darrel responds in a composed fashion.

"Back in my day we had child protective services to deal with situations like this. Every since that fourth world war nothing has been the same! But we still didn't have to put up with thieving brats like you!"

"Jerald stop!"

Darrel turned away from Mr. Peng.

"Sorry about your house sir," Darrel quietly spoke. He then walked away from the crowd and toward his apartment building with Manny following close behind.

As the two gained distance from Mr. Peng and the others Manny questioned his brother.

"Why didn't you tell him off Doggie? We both know you were at work all day. You couldn't have broken into his house."

"Yeah I know Manny."

Manny curled a frown on his face. He knew that whenever his brother called him by his real name that he was serious and not in a talkative mood.

"There's no need to fight with Mr. Peng over this," said Darrel.

"But you seemed so anxious when you asked if he yelled at me. Now he yelled at you and you just walked away."

"That's the point Manny. He can yell at me all he wants. That doesn't matter to me at all. But if he'd brought you into it then this would be a very different situation."

Manny's face showed confusion.

"I don't think I understand."

Darrel stopped walking. He looked down at Manny and laid his hand on the top of his head.

"One day you will Monkey," he said with a smile on his face.

Just then Mr. Peng began marching back toward the brothers.

"Boy!"

Darrel and Manny both turned to face him.

"Where have you been all day?"

"Work sir."

"And where exactly do you work?"

"I'm an apprentice electrician."

"Oh really? Show me your Kleins. My cousin is an electrician and he tells me every electrician has a pair. Let me see yours."

"Jerald this is ridiculous! Just drop it!" his wife yells.

"Let me see them boy!"

Darrel opened his tool bag and shuffled through his belongings. He had no idea what Kleins were but he looked as though he could find them if given time. He put his hands on a pair of wire cutters.

"Could this be them?" he thought as he closed his bag back up.

"I must have left them at work. Sorry but I should give a call to the office to find out if anyone's seen them," said Darrel while avoiding eye contact. He then scurried away from scene in a hurry.

Darrel rushed up the stairs outside his apartment and into the front door. Manny tagged behind leaving everyone else confused and curious. The crowd eventually departed as people returned to their homes.

That evening proved difficult for Darrel to weather. He stood leaning on his balcony rail while staring into the never ending hills of green. The California sunset made a perfect transition from the productive day into a ponderous night. Darrel swatted at his left arm.

"Looks like the mosquitoes are back."

Darrel lowered his arms and raised his head to take witness of the sun's last minutes of presence. The dusk sky guided his eyes to a particular spot at the base of the hills. He knew this area very well. It's where he practiced opening his Maerdym gates when he was alone.

Overtime his mind drifted. He eventually fell into deep thought...

"Is what I'm doing right? That girl, Tania. She said it was okay. It is okay, isn't it? After all it's for Manny. But still..."

Just then Darrel catches a glimpse of unusual movement downstairs.

"What the...? What's that guy doing? Could he be...?"

Darrel glanced through the glass sliding door to his living room. Manny was fast asleep on the couch with his hand in a bag of potato chips. He studied the clock on the wall that was displaying 2:15 AM.

"Two fifteen? How long have I been out here?

He looked back down at the earlier event.

"Wait! Where's that guy going? And what is he carrying? Of course, the real burglar!"

The mysterious figure whispered down the apartment streets with a sack over his shoulder. He had a mask over his face and jet black spiky hair.

"So how long you gonna follow me?"

"You're pretty observing."

Darrel stepped out of the shadows now that his cover was blown.

"What's goin on? Kind of suspicious hauling that bag around at two o clock in the morning."

"Just shut up. You know exactly what I'm doing. Now the situation can go many ways depending on your level of cooperation. Walk away. Trust me, you don't want to mess with me."

"Is that so? I think I'll take my chances. You're the one going around robbing houses."

"And so what if I am?"

"Your deeds are getting all the fingers pointed at me. It's time I cleared my name!"

Darrel dashed forward and delivered a punch to the thief's stomach. But to his surprise his fist was soaked in, water!

"You know once I had a bad dream that I was caught in a flood. There was nothing but water everywhere. Allow me to make my dream, your reality!"

"Maerdym? You're a chaser too!"

Chapter 3: Chaser Dual

"What's goin on?" Darrel wondered. "I never would have thought there'd be others able to use Maerdym. Who is this guy?"

"Surprised?"

The masked bandit grasped Darrel's wrist and flung him into the air. Darrel crashed into a trash dumpster making a large indent. He collected himself, shaking his head like a wet dog.

"Just who are you?" he asked.

"My name is Andre. And your name's going to be dead if you don't quit trying to be a hero."

Andre's torso began reforming from its aquatic state.

"He can turn his body into water. But it looked like it took him a minute to solidify." Darrel pried himself out of the dumpster's metal framing. "Looks like he struggles opening and closing gates too. Still, if his dream was a flood then I'm sure he's got a lot more water at his disposal. Can I beat him with speed?"

Darrel's light brown eyes began changing shades, slowly returning to their evergreen coloring from before. His chest lit up like a firework at its very moment of explosion. When the light died down he is seen wearing his previous crimson red vest.

"That can't be what I think it is," Andre uttered. "Those eyes, that vest, tell me, what is your name?"

The scene paused as Darrel raised his head.

"I am Darrel, Darrel Dustin."

Andre stood in awe at the statement. The wind began picking up as the two stood but yards away from each other.

"So the Dustin family isn't all gone after all huh? Or are you the last one?"

"Me and my brother are the last of the great Dustin family. Do you know now what you're really up against?"

"Ha-ha-ha-ha. And here I thought you were going to be a pushover. Guess I was wrong. Oh well, at least this should be more interesting then."

Darrel was surprised the knowledge of his heritage didn't make the thief surrender.

"So you being a Dustin confirms my suspicions. That vest you're wearing is the legendary Xavier's Vest."

"What do you know about my vest?"

"You're pretty ignorant to be a Dustin. You don't deserve that vest. Allow me to take it from you!"

Andre leaped forward with his arm rocketing at Darrel.

"Damn, he's fast!"

Andre powerfully grappled onto Darrel's neck. Darrel fought to resist, clutching the wrist that was choking his life away. The two wrestled to the ground with Andre still squeezing the breath from Darrel's throat.

"Damn think Darrel!" he told himself. "There must be a way to win!"

Darrel stretched out his free hand. It was quickly smothered in a glow with a luxurious flare. His dagger appeared once again. He used every ounce of his strength to thrust the dagger into Andre's neck. But his efforts were futile. The neck he presumed stabbing instantly liquefied before taking damage.

"HA! It's no use. Don't you get it by now? You're going to die!"

Darrel could feel his consciousness gradually slipping away like the grains in an hourglass.

"I have to do something! I have to..."

Darrel fell into a wake of darkness. He couldn't see what he saw, couldn't feel what he touched. The chaos began to fade from his perception. He found himself... nowhere.

"Are you in trouble Darrel?"

"What? Who's there?"

"Do you need me Darrel?"

"Who are you?"

"I am what you dreamt me to be Darrel."

"I can't see you. Where are you talking to me from?"

"I am hanging on the cliff of your desire, in the light of your insanity and the shadows of your beliefs."

"Wait, what?"

"You are running out of time Darrel. Do you require my assistance?"

"I... I... I do! Help me, please."

"Very well, young Dustin."

Darrel's eyes regained sight. His ears heard once more. He had returned to the fight.

"This is the end kid. Now, die!"

Darrel's grip on Andre's wrist loosened, until finally it released completely.

"That's it. Give up. I'll be taking that vest soon!"

Darrel fought the urge to let death take him away, but every second it grew stronger. But then! An outburst!

The palm of his hand suddenly unleashed hundreds of charging hounds with blood in their eyes. Like a broken fire hydrant, they spewed out his hand, swallowing the unsuspecting thief in the mist of their rage. With several wolves clenching onto Andre's limbs, his escape was impossible. They drove him back streaming their force of a thousand beasts! The wolves all had night black fur giving the pack of them an appearance of a horizontally charged dark waterfall. Their howls sent a spine chilling ring through the night air.

The wolves pounded the ground with their paws of might. At last the stream was cutoff. The bulk of the wolves vanished with a few remaining, pinning Andre to the ground.

At last Darrel rose.

"What... was... that?" Darrel spoke, still gasping for air. He rubbed his throat hoping to relieve some of the pain. He then stared cautiously at his palm.

Andre lay on the ground half conscious. The wolves growled and snarled while still holding him down.

One-by-one room lights throughout the apartment complex begin to kindle. By now some people are standing on their balconies viewing the battle between the two chasers.

Manny scurried down the stairs to check on his brother.

"Doggie!" he yelled.

Darrel turned to Manny who is now just a few feet away.

"Doggie, you okay?"

He straightened his posture before taking a deep breath.

"Yeah, I'm good. What are you doing out here? Go back inside."

Manny didn't respond. Instead he eyeballed his brother in concern. Darrel looked at Manny, then at the fallen Andre.

"Manny."

"Yeah?"

"How much did you see?"

"I was watchin from the window ever since you left. I'm sorry. You was actin weird so I faked bein sleep."

Darrel was silent. His expression was stone solid.

"Manny, listen, I know you're probably confused. Don't be scared. I'm still your broth-"

"-I'm not scared."

The older brother raised his eyes in shock.

"I've known for a while now. I used to watch you practice in the hills."

The thick tension broke as Darrel cracked a smile.

"Ha-ha you're a trip Monkey."

The two felt their nerves calming and both peered over at Andre on the ground. The wolves continued fading away until only one stood tall seemingly waiting on a command from Darrel.

"Doesn't she look familiar?"

"Who?"

"The dog over there, haven't we seen her before?" Manny said as he pointed at the remaining hound.

"I have a hard enough time remembering people. You expect me to remember animals too?"

Darrel began cautiously advancing toward Andre and the black hound. Neighbors gathered around the scene in hysteria. Their whispers steadily grew louder.

"They're both freaks like those families that ruined our world!"

"Someone call the cops!"

"Already done!"

"Good arrest them both!"

"Yeah Peng was right!"

Darrel towered over Andre, beaming at him as if he were diligently searching his soul.

"You know it's over right? Darrel questioned. "You're done."

"It's far from over kid. You may have beaten me, but there's bigger trouble ahead."

"I'm not afraid. I can escape from the cops, even if they blame the theft on me."

"It's not that."

"Then what?"

"You should understand now that there are more chasers outside of the Dustin bloodline. In fact, there are more chasers outside of the four families. One in particular you need to worry about is Max Stein."

"Max Stein?"

"Yeah. He's an extremely powerful chaser, a lot stronger than me. And since you're a Dustin, he'll be after you."

"How did you become a chaser?"

"Shut up! We don't have much time till the cops get here."

"Fine, just tell me about Max Stein."

"Listen. Before the fourth World War there was a small alliance made between the Dustin and Rector family."

"Rector family?"

"Just listen! The alliance formed the base of a new town, New Rialto. In the town there was a group of four exceptional chasers. The group called themselves Kombinajo. Kombinajo worked as mercenaries for both the Dustin and Rector family without either of them knowing that they were working for both families. When World War Four started, it pitted the two great families against each other and the Dustins eventually caught wind of Kombinajo's double-double agency. So they set them up with a fake mission and had them all killed. Although one chaser escaped, Max Stein. He went back to New Rialto, in search of allies to recruit. He wanted to take revenge on the Dustins for his comrade's murders."

"That explains why he'll be after me."

"But no one would help him. They were all either too scared, too weak, or didn't believe in his cause. So he left in anger. But a few weeks ago, he returned. He postponed his vengeance toward the Dustins. His new motivation was the complete annihilation of the people New Rialto."

"What the hell? He's sick!"

"Sick or not, he's killing all of us."

"So you're from New Rialto too."

"None of us can stop him. We can't go back to our town so most of us have nowhere to live and nothing to eat. Stealing was my only way to survive."

"Was? You talk as though those prison bars will be able to hold you."

"Wow you really are slow aren't you?"

Darrel stared in confusion.

"Getting locked up is going to be the best thing for me. I'll be safe. Stein can't get me there."

"I never thought of it that way. So in a way you wanted to lose this fight."

"No way, I tried to win, trust me. But I will admit that this makes a decent back up plan. He-he-he"

"Well here they come."

Police officers quickly flood the scene.

"You should know by now that Xavier's Vest will make you fast enough to get out of here."

"I'll need to grab Manny first."

"STOP AND PUT YOUR HANDS IN THE AIR!"

"Get out of here kid. And one more thing…"

"Yeah?"

"You're a chaser. Chasers stride forward, and they never look back."

Like lightning Darrel whips past everyone and scoops Manny up. He then vanishes with incredible speed.

Chapter 4: Runaways from Birth

"How you doing Monkey?"

"I'm okay. I should be askin you that. Please put me down Doggie. I know you're in pain."

"I'm fine don't worry."

"Ugh you always do this. You try to act all big and bad but you won't be fine at all if you die Doggie!"

Darrel came to a halt. He slowly bent his knees as Manny slid off his back.

"There, you happy now?" Darrel commented.

After hitting his feet Manny twisted his body around.

"Hmm, she's still followin us."

"You mean the mutt? Why do you keep calling it a she like you're sure it's a girl?"

"Because I AM a female," the wolf declared.

"WHAT THE!" the brothers shouted in complete surprise. "YOU CAN TALK?!"

"Of course I can talk. After all whos voice did you think you were hearing asking if you needed help Darrel?"

"Doggie, what is she talkin about?" Manny asked.

"Oh so it was you after all," said Darrel. "I knew I recognized your voice. But can you clear some things up for me? Starting with, who the hell are you?!"

"Interesting, young humans are extremely rude. If you must know, my name is-"

"-Pepper!" Manny blurted.

"What are you talking about now Monkey?"

"Don't you remember? Pepper, she looks just like Pepper, from a long time ago, remember?"

Darrel began strongly examining the hound.

"Wow you're right. I remember now. She looks just like one of those two dogs we rescued a couple of years ago."

"Bingo," the dog replied.

"Huh? That's crazy, you can't be Pepper. You came out of the palm of my hand."

"No, actually the gate you opened was NEAR the palm of your hand. I myself came to this world from Maerdym."

"That still doesn't explain how you can be Pepper and um, let me think, oh yeah, HOW YOU CAN TALK! I'm pretty damn sure the Pepper we found off the streets couldn't do that," Darrel implied.

"Indeed, but do you remember what happened the night after Pepper and Salt ran away?"

The brothers looked at each other in confusion.

"Specifically you Darrel."

"Uh, the only thing I can remember is a bad dream I had about what might happen to them."

"Precisely."

"You mean, you're my dream? Well that explains why you're from Maerdym. That's where all dreams go right?"

"Yes and you being a chaser, have the ability to access me at will. This power is further amplified due to Xavier's Vest. Do you remember when you were little? It was before Manny was born. You watched an episode of your favorite television show. Ninja Lobo Warriors was its name I believe?"

"Ha-ha oh yea I remember that show."

"When you slept, many nights you would dream of being a Ninja Lobo Warrior. You dreamed of wielding their coveted daggers with the gold wolf design on the blade."

"Like the one you had earlier Doggie!"

"I see now. So you are Pepper. Guess you could talk in my dream too. It all makes since now. So did you meet all of my dreams in Maerdym?"

"Yes I did. I was surprised to see your dream of being a famous country singer."

"Hey that was one time!"

Manny and Pepper laughed while Darrel stood embarrassed, eventually joining in the laughter himself.

Suddenly Pepper's nose began sniffing as if it picked up a strange new scent. She stopped laughing and wandered around the area as if her nose was guiding her somewhere.

"Pepper what's up? You smell something?" Darrel asked.

"Not something," Pepper answered. "Someone."

Manny moved closer to his brother as he spoke.

"Who is it Pepper?"

"I am not sure. But this scent is familiar. It must be from our previous setting."

"You mean the apartments?" Darrel asked.

"Indeed."

The bushes beside them began to ruffle as someone stepped out of them. It was a man with short brown hair and light skin. The lack of lighting made it difficult to distinguish any other physical traits.

"Who are you? And why are you following us? You've got about three seconds to answer buddy before this knife is in your throat!"

The lobo dagger appeared in Darrel's hand.

"Oh boy, it looks like I have to show you that form again huh? I'm not too fond of staying in that form for long, but I suppose it can't be helped."

The mysterious man closed his eyes and stood perfectly still. Just then his body lit up with a luxurious flare, burning with a heat fueled by lost imagination.

"Im... possible!" Darrel thought to himself.

"Do you two know him?"

"Yeah, that's..."

Before him and the others stood no other than...

"Mr. Peng!"

Chapter 5: Mr. Peng

The awkward silence broke as Peng spoke.

"Why does everyone look so surprised? Surely, being a chaser yourself, you knew that I was one too? After all, every chaser should be sharp and quick witted, should they not? You would have certainly known if another chaser lived within walking distance of you, right?"

"That's enough." Darrel interrupted. "What do you know about being a chaser anyw…" Darrel cut his sentence short, as he recapped on what he had just witnessed.

"Ah but you would have known, if you were truly a chaser," Peng continued. "You're still just a rookie."

"A rookie? Then how about we test that theory. I'll kill you, and then you can tell me if I'm still a rookie."

"Ah yes. And you should know plenty about killing, shouldn't you Darrel?"

Darrel froze. With all eyes on him, he froze.

"Doggie, what is he talkin about?"

Darrel hesitated then looked at his brother.

"It... It's nothing Manny!" Darrel began to think to himself. "Damn! He obviously knows more than I thought." He then returned to his conversation with Peng. "What do you want Peng? Why are you here?

"I merely want to talk. I have very important and valuable information for you."

Without feeling he had a choice, Darrel complied. "Fine, let's talk alone. Pepper you stay here with Manny."

"Understood."

"Doggie!"

"I'm not going to be gone long Monkey."

"I know but, just watch your back okay?"

"Always."

Darrel and Peng slowly began walking away from the others. Darrel watched Peng closely the entire way. Peng looked forward calmly as if he knew exactly what was about to happen.

"Okay this is far enough," Darrel commanded.

"If that is what you wish."

"Now, tell me everything you know."

"Well for starters I know you're not an electrician. I also know that what you really do wouldn't be seen as very admirable to your little brother."

"Enough! How did you find out?"

"I've been watching you for a long time now Darrel. Your moves were constantly watched by me, every since I saw you in the hills."

"So that's how you know about me being a chaser."

"Yes but even before I witnessed your practices, I knew there was something different about you. Even now I sense something in you different than an average chaser."

"Like what?"

"I'm not sure yet, and I fear I won't be sure for a while. But this feeling has lead me hear, to fulfill this task."

"What task?"

"The task of teaching you, to be the chaser to save this world!"

Darrel froze yet again.

"You must be joking. Save this world from what? And why me?"

"Like I said before, I don't know myself. But in time everything will become clearer to the both of us."

"Fine, then why don't you start by telling me about yourself? Exactly who are you really?"

"In due time Darrel. But first I will tell you about the person *YOU* really are. First and foremost, you are of one of the four great families."

"That's the same thing that Andre guy was saying. If there are four families, then who are the other three?"

"If you really want to know, then I must take you back... to when the power was passed down."

The Time Before part 3: The Four Families

"Why have you brought me here Xavier?" Professor Save asked. "What is this place?"

Xavier stepped closer to Save, showing the dramatic difference in their size. Xavier stood tall with a muscular build. He was dark skinned with short cut hair. His camouflage suit covered his whole body other than his feet which wore light brown boots.

"This is the army's base fifty one Save."

"Why did the army tell you to bring me here? What do they want with me? I'm just a university professor!"

"You and I both know you are more than that Save. And the army didn't tell me to bring you here. This meeting is of my own personal reasoning."

"You don't mean... Is this about Maerdym? Xavier those are just theories! I appreciate your belief and support, but even if such a world existed, I have yet to control it. Now we must forget about Maerdym right now and figure out a way to stop this attack!"

"Okay, fine. But tell me one thing. Who exactly is attacking America Save?"

"The... the..."

"Just as I thought, you can't lie to me, because you can't lie to yourself. You know there is a darker culprit behind this assault. And you also know that Maerdym is the only thing we have to stop it! The ammo belongs to our surrounding countries but someone, or something else pulled the trigger! If you won't listen to me than listen to yourself!"

"YOU listen to YOUR self Xavier! The world as we know it is in turmoil and you want to talk about some fairy tale?" Save screamed, flashing back to the student's comment earlier. "Now tell me where Glen and Sarah are!"

"We put them in the other room. Would you rather them here?"

"I would."

"Fine. BRING THEM IN PRIVATE WAYANS." Xavier shouted.

Xavier's partner presses the open button. The sliding doors opened and Sarah and Glen barged in. Sarah stomped her way over to Xavier in a heated fury.

"Who do you think you are?!" she yelled. "I don't care if you're an army hoocko! You have no right to be kidnapping people like this! And what the hell did you do to the professor? I swear, if you hurt him I'm gonna-"

"-Sarah!" Save shouted.

"WHAT!?"

"Uh, he's not our enemy. He wouldn't hurt either of us. This is... my brother... Xavier Dustin.

Everyone paused as if time itself took a break.

"Your brother, professor?" Glen asked.

"Yes Glen." He answered.

"You expect us to believe that? I mean I know sometimes, in fact a lot of the times now days, brothers don't look alike. But you two look like exact opposites."

"I never told you this Sarah, but I'm adopted."

Xavier spoke, "I don't mean to sound rude-"

"-Oh that boat has sailed pendejo!" Sarah exclaimed.

After clearing his throat, Xavier continues. "Anyways, like I was saying, my family found Save when he was an infant. He was in a dark alley all alone and covered in clothes much too big for him. We took him in as our own, not knowing much about him at all. He was alone when we found him. I was very young at the time but I remember it vividly. All we had to go off of was a note left with him."

"What was on the note?" the curious Glen inquired.

"All it said was, call me Save, and nothing else. From that moment we did as the letter asked, not even giving Save our family name."

"Is this true Save?" Sarah remarked.

"Yes," Save answered with little hesitation.

"Wow. I'm sorry for what I said earlier Xavier."

"It's fine. But I feel I am the one who owes the apology, to you my brother."

"What could you possibly have to apologize to me about Xavier? You've done so much for me."

"No, I'm afraid I've hidden something from you all these years Save. When we found you, the letter, had a bit more written on it."

"What are you talking about Xavier... Xavier?"

"The note said more than what we've revealed to you. It said that, of the puzzle, you are the Saver Piece."

"But what does that mean?"

Xavier turned his back to the others as he spoke.

"It took me a while to figure it out myself. But after reading your books on Maerdym, I came to a realization. Growing up with you as kids, I could always tell you were different. Like you were meant for something bigger, something no human could ever fathom. I could see it in your writing as well. It's as if you were unknowingly prophesying... the truth. The truth to everything. Your findings on Maerdym revolved around an idea that there were beings on this planet meant to work together in order to reel it out of this darkness. Work together, like pieces to a puzzle. And you Save, are the Saver Piece.

"The, Saver Piece?" Save repeated.

Everyone's attention was on the professor. No one blinked, as if they were all waiting for a response from him.

"What I speak is confirmed Save."

Xavier reached in his suit pocket and pulled out a ragged piece of paper.

"It's all in this note. Just as I said."

"You kept that all this time?" Save asked.

"I knew this day would come Save. Even back then I knew your destiny would require you to read this letter."

Xavier handed the tattered note to Save with hesitation. Save slowly opened the parcel, careful enough not to rip it. His eyes paced over it in a steady rhythm.

"This is incredible."

"What is it Save?" Sarah wondered.

"What are you thinking professor?" Glen followed.

"I've been studying Maerdym for so long. And I will admit there were many times when I questioned everything I believed in. I asked myself if I'd lost all sanity. But now, I have never been so... so certain."

"We have little time left brother. The world needs you. Where do you want to go? The army has the quickest fast-tran shuttles invented. Just name where you want to go."

Save stood still in deep thought.

"How far do your shuttles reach?"

"We can go anywhere in the U.S. boundaries in a matter of minutes."

"Wow that fast?!" Sarah shouted.

"In that case, all I need is somewhere I can focus. Somewhere with no interruptions."

"Like the top of a mountain?" Glen suggested.

"Yes! That would be perfect. What do you think Xavier? Can you make that happen?"

"I'm on it," Xavier says while pulling out his cell phone. "Yes, this is Sergeant Dustin. Have me a helicopter at the base of Mt. St. Helens immediately... Don't ask questions! This is an emergency!... Okay good. We must leave immediately Save," said Xavier as he put his phone away.

"Yeah, right. I'm leaving now Sarah, Glen, stay safe. And whatever happens, I appreciate you both for your friendship."

"Uh friendship?" Sarah announces as she makes her way over to Save. With no hesitation she gives him an unexpected kiss on the lips. "I know you can do it Save."

"Good luck professor."

"Thanks Glen," Save said while he tried to cool down from the sign of affection. "And thank you too," he spoke toward Sarah. "Maybe when I get back I can get some more of that ha-ha."

"Oh trust me, when you get back you're gonna be getting more than that," Sarah says in a seductive tone. Save's face shines bright red.

"Uh, yes well that's enough Save we have to make our leave."

"Oh yes of course. Goodbye you two."

With that the brothers leave and make their way to the base of the St. Helens. The helicopter is waiting for them as planned and they quickly board it and make their way near the top. The wind is strong and voices are barely hearable.

"It's all up to you now Save!" Xavier yells through the wind.

Save is calm and relaxed. His body shows no movement and his breaths are even as can be.

"Focus Save," Save thinks to himself. "You can do this. There's no one else to save us. It's now or never."

Xavier glances at his watch.

"Oh no! Only five minutes till impact!

Save stays relaxed. He then raises his hands to the sky. The missiles become visible through the clouds. Save extends his arms apart. He shows no fear to death staring him straight in the eyes.

The sky lights up! All around there is a new light. A luxurious flare, burning with a heat fueled by lost imagination. All of a sudden a giant gaping hole in the sky forms. It's black and filled with endless nothingness. It appears to be absorbent, sucking in all the clouds around it. An enormous drain is pulling everything in the sky into a void of disappearance. Soon the destructive missiles become a part of this mass. They all slowly course straight into the hole, completely vanishing out of existence.

The black hole faded away inch by inch until it was gone entirely. Save fell to his knees in exhaust. Xavier stood frozen in amazement as he opened his mouth to speak.

"You... you did it. Save you did it! You saved us all!"

Save was quiet. He had not yet pulled himself together after his ordeal.

"You okay?"

"Yeah, I'm okay," Save replied as he rose again to his feet.

"It's been one hell of a day hasn't it?"

"Yeah. What do you think people will say about the missiles disappearing?"

"I don't think that will be as much of an issue. The U.S. won't accept this. They're going to fight back Save. But we will cross that bridge when we get there. For now, you and I must focus on why those weapons of mass destruction were launched in the first place."

"How will we find that out?"

"We? You already know. Search your thoughts. Somehow this power, this knowledge is already in your head. What do you see?"

After taking a brief pause to gather his thoughts, Save responds. "There is a greater evil at work. I'm not sure what it is exactly, but I know it isn't human. But I fear…"

"What is it? Tell me."

"I fear I won't be able to stop it."

"What do you mean? If not you than who? You just need to learn how to master Maerdym. But then again, who would teach you?"

"I have someone in mind."

"It's impossible to teach something you don't know. And you're the only one who can use Maerdym! You'll just have to train on your own."

"No, no I have someone in mind."

"Save?"

"Xavier, you just focus on keeping the worlds order. I fear we've won the battle, but the war has just begun."

Save couldn't have chosen his words more perfectly. Soon after the events on that day the third world war in history commenced. Many smaller counties were being destroyed in the shockwave of this record shattering battle. It seemed there was no end in sight. No one could end the war, because no one was sure how it really began. For two years countless lives were lost. But in these two years, a hero was emerging...

"You look tired my boy."

"Yes, I've been up all night."

"Still working on that book eh?"

"Ha-ha, it's more than a book sensei. This piece of writing can change the world!"

"Hmm. Change the world you say? And here I've been throwing my books in the closet all this time. When in actuality I've been throwing the world in my closet."

"HA-HA-HA. Sensei you're too much. Raiyu Nguyen, the funniest teacher on the planet earth."

"I'm sure I'd be the funniest in Maerdym also, young Save."

"Probably so sensei, I want to thank you again for training me all this time. I just hope I haven't been too much of a bother."

"You know you say that every day. The next time you say it, you WILL be a bother. Besides, it wasn't as difficult as you made it to be. Once you enlightened me on the basics of Maerdym mastery, it was simple creating a training plan for you."

"I had faith in you sensei. That's why I came here two years ago."

"Well I suspected you weren't flying all the way to Korea Prime to have tea and sausage links."

Raiyu rose to the window above head.

"But many days I wonder…"

"What troubles you sensei?"

"Is this enough?"

Save's gaze deepened toward his teacher, who is now lost in thought.

"Yes, I agree."

"Though I did not witness it myself, I believe every word of you saving the states once. But… Even if you once again save those in need. When will the fighting end? As long as mankind recognizes their differences before their similarities, they will never evolve."

"Sensei."

Raiyu leaned on the railing under his window seal. His old brittle legs were already growing tired from his few moments of standing. The rising sun gleamed off of his bare head. His long gray beard reached the floor even if he had been on his toes.

"Save my boy."

"Yes? Please, tell me."

"We as humans must ascend beyond this evil."

"But, how?"

"That question may never be answered young one. But enough of that talk. Tell me again about your book."

"Like I said it's much more than a book. I've written a lot of books on Maerdym, but this is far from being in their category."

"Oh?"

"Yes indeed."

"How so?"

"Well you see, two years ago, I was told something by my brother."

"Ah how is your brother these days?"

"He's fine sensei; I talk to him every day, but-"

"-Oh and what of your wife?"

"Sarah is doing fine too sensei. Anyways-"

"When are you two going to have some kids?"

"We've been, uh trying sensei," Save said while his face blushed.

"And that boy. Uh what was his name again?"

"Glen, sensei. His name is Glen and his life is going well. Now can I please continue my story?"

"Story?"

"RAIYU SENSEI!"

"Relax my boy. I'm only hockooing around with you."

"Yes well, hockooing aside, like I was saying. Two years ago Xavier told me something that really opened my eyes. My entire life I held this knowledge that wasn't exactly logical to the average person. But to me, all of it made perfect sense. I never knew the meaning behind these thoughts until I found out I was the Saver Piece."

"That still doesn't explain the book."

"This, book as you call it, holds all of that information. Information about the past, and a glimpse into our world's possible future. I leave this book, no this prophecy for the next generation. Hopefully they will be able to heed my warnings, and receive my blessings. I just pray the prophecy never falls into the wrong hands. Not even I can tell what would happen then."

"Interesting, but does this prophecy have a name?"

Save's stare pointed directly at Raiyu.

"Yes," Save responded as his brother's word floated in his memories.

"It's as if you were unknowingly prophesying… the truth. The truth to everything," he remembered Xavier saying.

"Truth. That is its name."

"Truth you say. Ha I like it."

"I had a feeling you would," Save remarked with a smile on his face.

Not long after the completion of Truth, World War Three intensified. The fighting left a massive head count across countless regions. At last the time came for the Saver Piece to make his move.

Save stood tall in the middle of a desert wasteland. The sand twisters were kicking up around him. His company consisted of those closest to him,

Glen Heard, Sarah Rector, Xavier Dustin, and Raiyu Nguyen.

"Before we begin I'd like to start by saying it feels really good to have the four people I love the most here together for the very first time," Save opened. "Also, I know this isn't the most ideal place to be gathering but according to my brother Xavier, this is where the next battle will go down. I feel it appropriate for you all to be here and witness what I am about to do."

"We aren't the only ones watching Save," Xavier verbalized. "There are many who wish to see if the rumors of you are true. I'm sure all of us here know by now that spectators a few years ago linked the failed attack on America to this man here. They saw you open the black hole in the sky. And they're watching us now waiting on another miracle."

Sarah walked up to Save. She grabbed his hand and focused her eye contact on him.

"Save, where is Truth?"

"It's in a safe place."

"What do you mean in a safe place?" Glen said entering the conversation. "No place is safe now Professor. We're at war!"

"Earth is at war Glen."

"How does that change anything?"

"Silence young Glen," Raiyu interrupted. "Continue my boy."

Save smiled at Glen to ease his worry. He then continued to speak.

"The reason I needed the four of you here with no one else is because in my prophecy, I wrote something that surprised even myself."

"What is it honey?"

"This is extremely big news. I... Am not the only capable of using Maerdym. You all can learn too!"

The four stood with unchanged expressions.

"Aren't you all surprised?"

"I think I can speak for all of us when I say, nothing surprises us with you anymore brother," Xavier spoke.

A contagious smile spread to everyone in the group.

"Well how do we learn it?" Glen asked.

"The same way I trained for two years. Maerdym is mastered through four key attributes. Power, control, depth, and understanding. By utilizing these four, you can become an excellent chaser."

"Chaser?"

"Oh yeah. It's what I call one who uses Maerdym. The same way one chases their dreams. You will chase yours. You will all be chasers. And I will teach you the ways of Maerdym. I only ask that you teach Maerdym only to those within your family. From this day on, you are... The Four Great Families.

Chapter 5 continued

"So that's who the four families are?"

"Yes, the power of Maerdym was passed down that day to your family along with three others."

"Wait a minute, what were their names again?"

"The families are Dustin, Heard, Nguyen, and Rector."

"Did you say Rector? I knew that's what I heard before."

"What about it?"

"Nothing... You still haven't told me about yourself," Darrel said as he changed the subject. "If you wanna roll with us you're going to have to let me in on exactly who you are."

"Don't you think this is information Manny should be told as well?"

"...Fine, but we stay away from any talk about me working for Triple Hawk got it?"

"Understood."

Darrel and Peng reunited with the others.

"Darrel I'm afraid my time is drawing thin," Pepper said immediately.

"What are talking about?"

"My time here in the real world is limited. I must return to my dream form in Maerdym."

"Oh yeah, sure. Thanks a lot Pepper."

"Whenever you need me, I am but a world away," Pepper speaks her last words before fading away.

"Ha-ha Pepper is funny. She told me stories of how she would poop in our shoes and made it look like it was Salt's fault."

"You know Manny, she would be able to stay longer and tell you more funny stories if your brother had more control as a chaser."

"Okay Peng we get it!"

"Doggie, what's a chaser?"

"Well, it's like this. You remember all that weird stuff you saw earlier? Well it all came from a dream world called Maerdym. Chasers are people who can open gates to Maerdym. Get it?"

"Um kind of. So how do you become a better chaser?"

"That's what Mr. Peng is here to tell us. Isn't that right Peng?"

"Maerdym is mastered through four attributes, power, control, depth, and understanding. It would appear that power comes natural to you Darrel, but you must train in the other categories in order to truly become stronger."

"So does that mean Mr. Peng is going to train you Doggie?"

"Yeah I guess, for now."

"Than it's settled! From now on we travel together!"

"And where exactly are we going?" Darrel asked.

"Why to the east of course!"

"Why the east?"

"Because that is where it is believed the Saver Piece hid Truth."

"Truth?" Manny asked.

"Yes it's the prophecy left by the Saver Piece himself."

"Wait! Just how did this go from you training me to looking for a book all the way in the East?"

"The entire purpose of this all is for the world to be saved. And we need Truth in order to do that."

"That's another thing. What are we saving the world FROM?"

"Not even I have all the answers Darrel."

Darrel suddenly hears a rumbling sound from below.

"Well before we do anything we're getting something to eat. Manny is starving. There's a Burger Stan down the street.

Chapter 6: Trouble at the Burger Stan

Darrel, Manny, and Peng walked through the yellow arcs into the Burger Stan. They immediately noticed that it was an older model due to the lack of personal seating booths. The sun was beginning its journey across the sky, but it was still very early in the morning so there were not many people out.

"I suppose I owe you two a background check don't I?" Peng questioned.

"Damn straight you do," Darrel answered.

"Well I'll try to make this quick. I am from Korea Prime. You see years ago there was a North Korea and a South Korea, but during the times of peace, they merged and became Korea Prime. I lived in a temple known as Maze. There I was taught the ways of Maerdym, but I was taught never to use my power to kill, no matter what."

"If that's the case, than why aren't you still in Korea? What brought you to the states?"

"Well basically I went on a trip and when I came back everyone in the temple was dead. End of story, wow I'm hungry! Aren't you?"

The brothers looked at each other and shrugged their shoulders. They were both thinking the same thing, when it came to death sometimes it was best to leave it alone.

Darrel drifted into a deep gaze at the sunrise.

"Doggie aren't we gonna order?"

"What? Oh yeah."

"The sun seems to interest you Darrel," Peng commented.

"Yeah, I guess you could say that. A little while ago I had a dream I was carrying the sun on my back. That was around the time life seemed to be piling troubles on me back and forth."

"You over analyze things too much Darrel. Much like how you pause whenever I say the word Rector."

Manny looked up in surprise. "Rector? That was Erica's last name wasn't it Doggie?"

"Erica? And just who might that be?"

"Nobody!" Darrel shouted, catching the attention of the few people in the store. "Let's just order our food. Manny put your order code in," he said trying to calm himself down. He looked around the room at the eyes that were on him. "What the?" he thought to himself as he noticed something peculiar.

"Well I guess I will stay off that subject," Peng told him. "Either way, I'm going to go to the bathroom," he said as he made his way to the restrooms.

"Hmm, I think I want the chicken nuggets. What are you gonna get Doggie? Doggie?"

Darrel's head was facing his brother but his eyes were glued to the individual he noticed earlier. Manny turned to see who he was staring at this whole time.

It was a shady character with dark sun glasses on. His hair was slicked back and the suit he wore made him look like he was supposed to be in a business meeting. He sipped his coffee very slowly, as if he were in no hurry to leave. The only noticeable feature about him was the symbol on his chest, three gold birds.

"There's no mistake. That's definitely the symbol of Triple Hawk!" Darrel pondered. "This guy must be a recruiter. Meaning he's after somebody here, but who?"

Darrel surveyed the room. Apart from Manny, himself, and the recruiter, there were four other bodies in the room. The manager walking around asking if anyone needed help ordering, an older lady who could barely lift her hand to press the buttons, a young woman who looked about Darrel's age with red streaked brown hair and a slim body with chestnut colored skin, and a young man also around the same age with bright blonde hair whisked to the back and two long bangs hanging in his light blue eyes.

"Doggie didn't you say we were gonna order?"

Darrel's attention could not be grabbed.

"So have you guys ordered yet?"

Both brothers look toward Peng who was just coming out of the bathroom, but it wasn't the same face they saw going in.

"You changed back to your other body Mr. Peng?" Manny asked.

"Oh yeah, this body is much more comfortable, especially after being confined to my Jerald body for so long."

"What is this one called?"

"You can call it my Johnny body."

"Oh okay. Well can I still call you Mr. Peng?"

"Ha-ha of course Manny," Peng looked over at Darrel. "Darrel is something bothering you?"

Darrel lead Peng's eyes to the recruiter he'd been staring at. Peng immediately noticed the Triple Hawk symbol.

"HI! Can I help you gentlemen?" said the manager out of nowhere. "I noticed you've been at this ordering console for a while now. Do you need help? Or maybe it isn't working properly?"

"No we're fine, just deciding on what to get," Darrel replied.

"Alright, well if you need me just give me a shout out."

"HEY WHAT'S THE DEAL YOU BASTARD?!" screamed the voice of a young lady.

"Um excuse me ma'am?"

The brown haired girl from before storms to the other side of the restaurant to confront the manager. Her intimidating stare somewhat took away from her natural attractiveness. Her curly brown head of hair bounced wildly as she dashed across the room.

"Don't excuse me! My grandmotha has been waitin for half an hour for some damn help! I know you saw her over here! She can't even lift her arm to touch the screen!"

The elderly lady looks over at them confused.

"Um young lady-" the old lady says.

"-Not now grandma I'm stickin up for ya! Now tell me you didn't notice her over here!"

"I... I'm sorry. I thought she already ordered," the manager replies as his body trembles in fear.

"So what you callin me a liar? You wanna fight or something?"

"What? No! How about I get you both a complimentary desert."

"So what you sayin you can buy me now? Just what the hell do ya take me for huh? No screw that lets fight!" the girl yelled while raising her fists toward the frightened worker.

"Hey how about we all just calm down," Darrel intervened.

"What you want some too tough guy? C'mon I'll take the both of ya!"

"Let's just take it easy ma'am I'm sure we can work this out," the manager says as he gently rests his hand on her shoulder.

"What the?! Did I say you can touch me? That's it you're dead!

The chocolate haired girl punches the manager straight in the nose. He hits the floor like a dead weight. Blood runs through his fingers as he clenches his face.

"What the hell! She broke my freaking nose!"

Everyone in the restaurant rises to their feet.

"That girl's got some bite behind that bark," Peng commented with a chuckle.

"I'm suing your socks off kid!" the manager yelled as he tried to control the bleeding.

"Sue me? What kind of man are you anyways huh? A real man would fight me! Ugh you guys are borin, forget it I'm just gonna take this whole store down!"

"What are you talking about?" the blonde guy in the back yells.

"I mean this! VIOLET BREATH!"

The girl took in a deep breath. Her chest expanded before everyone's eyes.

"Doggie, let's get away!"

"What do you mean? We don't even know what she's doing."

"Doggie look!"

Maerdym light mist seeped from the girl's tightly shut jaw.

"Darrel, Manny she's opening a gate in her stomach! Get out of the way!"

"Damn it! Manny run!"

Those around the girl quickly dash away from her. She then releases the breath she'd been holding all at once. Waves of purple shaded flames burst from her mouth engulfing everything around her. Soon the entire interior of the Burger Stan is set ablaze! Darrel and the others struggle to find each other in all the commotion.

"Monkey where are you!"

"Doggie!"

"Damn it where is he?" Darrel desperately wondered.

Darrel's eyes fade to green. His red vest appears as well.

"Looks like it's time to get out of here," the fire starter claims as she makes her way to the exit, but before she gets out she notices someone on the floor.

"Doggie help!"

Manny is on the ground with a piece of wood lying on his leg. The wood is much too big for him to move himself.

"C'mon kid, no reason for you to get caught up in this too," the girl says while moving the wood and throwing Manny over her shoulder.

"Wait what are you doin? Put me down! Doggie!"

"Shut up kid I'm savin you! What's your name kid?"

"Um, Manny."

"Alright Manny, I'm Karina. Nice to meet ya. Now hold on tight!"

Karina bent her legs and thrusts with a powerful leap toward the ceiling. She and Manny brace for impact but break through the ceiling with ease. They both are soon out of sight.

Darrel continues to search for his brother.

"Manny! Manny answer me!"

"The girl took your brother."

"What? Who are you? Wait you're!"

The man with the Triple Hawk symbol has now appeared in front of Darrel.

"I know you know what I do Darrel Dustin. I am a recruiter for Triple Hawk. I also know that you have your own affiliation with Triple Hawk. If you want your brother back I'm the only one who knows where Karina stays. I've been tracking her for some time now."

"This is dumb! Lately I've had to trust everyone! This is becoming too much. I swear if you're lying to me I'm gonna make you wish you would have stayed here and burned!"

"I guess that blonde kid made his way out, but I got everyone else out of here," says Peng as he returns from helping the others.

"Good. This recruiter guy is going to lead us to Manny. He better."

"Just follow me."

The three of them leap out of the same hole left by Karina, leaving behind a scene of complete destruction. They have no time to look back, Manny is up ahead.

Chapter 7: The Whispers Ignite

"Where are we goin?" Manny asked.

"Don't worry kid I aint gonna hurt ya."

"I know that, or else you wouldn't have saved me back then."

"You're a smart little kid aren't ya?"

"But I want to know where we're goin. Um, please Ms. Karina."

"Hey don't start throwin the Ms. around kid I'm only seventeen!"

"I'm sorry I was just trying to be respectful like my brother tells me to be to strangers."

"Strangers huh? Well let's see, your name is Manny, and what's my name?"

"Karina."

"There we aint strangers no more."

"Ha-ha-ha okay. I like you Karina. Do you want to be friends?"

"Uh yeah sure. Yeah, yeah we can be friends."

"So um Karina."

"Yeah?"

"Why were you so mad at everybody back there?"

Karina stopped.

"We're here," she said as though embarrassed to be there.

"Where is this?

"My home."

Manny looked ahead. What he saw shocked him, a trashy old abandoned shack on the edge of a lake. The grass was green in certain areas but the rest was dead and there was a broken bridge on the other side of the lake.

"Home sweet home," Karina said with sarcasm. "Why don't you call your brother to come pick you up?"

"But I don't have a phone or anything."

"Oh I thought you would have one. Well I guess we got us a little situation don't we? You hungry?"

"Very hungry!"

"Here chow down."

Karina reached in her pocket and tossed Manny a small burger still in its wrapper.

"Wow thanks."

"Yeah I jacked it from the machines in the back before you and ya brotha got there. It was my back up plan for findin a fight in that joint."

"But, why?" Manny asked with a mouth full of food.

"Why what?" Karina asked as she took out another burger from her pocket.

"Why do you like to fight so much?"

"You really want to know?"

"Yes."

Karina stopped eating her burger and looked at Manny.

Meanwhile Darrel and the others are on their way to confront Karina. They leap from the rooftops of buildings and houses at incredible speed.

"How far is it uh… What did you say your name was again?" Darrel asked the mystery man.

"I didn't."

"We're going to need a name recruiter," Darrel demanded.

"And perhaps a reason why you're helping us," Peng added.

"You can call me Ken. And as for my reason, well let's just say we have the same objective."

"Let's get one thing straight Ken, just because we both associate ourselves with Triple Hawk, does not make us similar in any way!"

"You'd be surprised."

Out of nowhere someone appears in front of the group. They all stop like they hit a red light on a highway.

"Stop right there. I need to ask you a few questions before any of you go any further," the man speaks.

"What? Just who the... wait weren't you just in that Burger Stan a minute ago?" Darrel asked.

"Yes, he is the blonde boy I couldn't find. I'm glad to see he made it out okay."

"Yeah but what the hell is he doing here? Who do you think you are stopping us like this? We're in a hurry so move or I'll make you move!"

"Good."

"What?"

"That's the answer I wanted to hear from you."

"From me? Do you know me from somewhere or something? Answer quick, I've got to go save my brother."

"No I don't know you. But I do know who you are."

"You do realize that made no sense right?"

"My name is Kyle Morgan. And I know you're a Dustin. I can tell from the eyes and your vest."

Darrel stopped talking in shock. After a minute of thinking to himself he clicked back on like a light bulb.

"So it's you."

"You know me?"

"I had a feeling we would meet. This suits me just fine. You hate all Dustins right? So if I get rid of you now I won't have to worry about you hurting my brother, Max Stein!"

"Max Stein? Sorry but you've got the wrong guy. Although, Max Stein is the reason why I hate Dustins."

"Just what are you talking about? If you're not Stein than who are you?"

"Darrel we need to leave. Every moment could be crucial," Peng pointed out.

"I already told you. You're not going anywhere. Now that I know what you are, we have business to handle. I see you know who Max is. And hopefully you know the situation right now in New Rialto."

"Yeah, Stein is killing off all the people of New Rialto."

"He's killing all of MY people! New Rialto has been my home for as long as I can remember! If it wasn't for you damn Dustins, it would still be my home!"

"Oh… I think I understand now."

"Do you?"

"Yeah, I understand that you want revenge on my family for killing Kombinajo and starting this Max Stein massacre."

"So, you do understand."

"Yeah, but I also understand something else."

"Oh yeah? What's that?"

"I understand that you're making a big mistake by fighting me."

"I expected as much from a Dustin. Your whole family has always been cocky! Well today I'm going to show how you're not as high and mighty as you think!"

"Fine, but it's not that."

"What?"

"If you really want to avenge those you've lost, fighting me will prove nothing! You should be getting stronger so that one day you could challenge Stein himself! AND THEN you would be extracting your revenge! Instead of picking a fight with me you should be focusing your energy on your real target!"

"Darrel calm down," Peng advises.

"To hell with calming down! This is what he needs to here!"

"Shut up," Kyle whispered.

All three men turn to Kyle in wonder.

"Just, SHUT UP!" This time Kyle yells to the top of his lungs. His fists are balled up tight enough to snap a normal person's bone in half. His face is glowing bright red and his teeth are clenched shut. All of a sudden dark rain clouds begin to form over head.

"There was no rain in the forecast," Ken comments.

"These are no ordinary clouds," Peng replies. "Look closer."

Ken and Darrel stare at the clouds that grow darker by the second. They see a glimmer of Maerdym light shining through.

"After he killed my mother and father, it's rained in every dream I've had thus far. Now allow me to show your brother the pain of losing a loved one!"

Kyle darted toward Darrel at full speed! The rain immediately began pouring down as if someone had turned on the sky's faucet.

"Don't just stand there Dustin! I'm coming at you! Defend yourself!"

Darrel struggled to see in front of him. The rain had grown so thick that it altered his line of sight. Out of nowhere, Kyle's fist strikes heavily on Darrel's face. Blood flies from his nose. Darrel returns with a blow of his own. Peng and Ken stand watch as the two exchange punches and kicks.

"They're both pretty skilled," Ken claims. "You must've taught the Dustin well, Peng."

"I actually haven't gotten the chance to yet. Wait, how did you know my name?"

Darrel and Kyle continue doing battle on the rooftops of south Corona. The rain is pounding their skin but it doesn't seem to bother them at all.

"We should go look for his brother," Ken says ignoring Peng's previous question. "Karina is a very quick tempered girl."

"You seem to know a lot about us all."

"I am a recruiter. It's my job to know a lot about certain people."

"Is that what you're going to tell me?"

"What are you insinuating?"

"Nothing, for now. But you're right; we need to go find Manny."

There is a break in the fight as the two chasers catch their breath.

"Darrel we're going to go on ahead while you handle things here!" Peng shouts.

"Yeah good idea. But be careful with that guy, and Ken."

"Hmm?"

"Remember what I told you. Bring him back, or I'll make you pay!"

"Understood."

With that the two vanish out of sight of Darrel and Kyle.

"Don't let me down Peng, please."

"Well looks like we're all alone now. Are you ready to go all out Dustin?"

"Let's do it blondie."

The rivals stare each other down intensely. Elsewhere Karina and Manny converse on other matters.

"Manny do you know where Brazil is?"

"Um, no. But my brother has told me about it. He says there isn't much left of it, just like a lot of countries after World War Four."

"Yeah, well before it was completely destroyed, it was my home."

"Did you like it there?"

"Oh yeah. I loved it. I had all my family with me."

"So why did you move?"

"It aint that simple kid. Ya see I grew up with my pops and six brothas. I was the only girl, not to mention I was the youngest in the family. My ma died when I was too young to rememba. When the war started I lost the rest of my family too. They all went to war and wouldn't let me fight at all, even though they raised me as a fighta my whole life. I was only a bit older then you but I knew I could handle myself on the battlefield."

"So that's why you like to fight so much."

"My family raised me to be tough, but the day they died I wasn't tough at all. Nobody came home, so I went out lookin for them. But Instead, I found trouble. A soldier, I aint sure if he was a chaser or not. I didn't know what side he was fightin for and I guess he wondered the same about me. That must have been why he attacked me. All my trainin with my pops and brothas went down the drain. I tried fightin back but my body just froze. I knew for sure I was going to die."

"What happened?"

"Well, the memory is kind of blurry but, I remember a man came out of nowhere. He was tall and… and… to be honest he kind of looked like you kid. I know that must sound crazy. Maybe my memories' worse than I thought. But there is one thing I'll never forget. He was ridin a dark purple dragon. I'm pretty sure this guy was a chaser. He saved me and all I could do was feint like a wimp. When I came to he was watchin over me. He told me that my family was gone. Then he said I was no longer in Brazil. I was in America. He started talkin some more but couldn't finish. Turns out someone was followin him and tried to take him out then and there. I don't know if he made it out alive or not. All I did was run. And I kept runnin…"

Manny watched Karina as she got up and walked across the room.

"What are you doin?" he asked.

"Makin some stew. I aint got much ingredients right now but I'll steal some more later."

"But we ate already. Are you still hungry?"

"What you trying to call me fat kid? Ha-ha I'm kiddin. This is for your brotha when he gets here."

"But how do you know he'll be able to find us?"

Karina put down her pot for a brief pause.

"When I saw your brotha look at you and when I heard him scream your name when he couldn't find you in the fire… It reminded me of how my family used to look at me and how they told me not to worry as they left for war. I saw the same love in his eyes, the same selfless care for you. Ya know what I mean kid?"

"Sometimes it scares me though."

"What do ya mean?"

"Like, I don't want him to care about only me. I want him to care about himself too."

"Has he always been that way?"

"No, there used to be another person he cared about a lot. We were so happy, the three of us."

"What happened?"

"Well, one day I woke up, and she was gone."

"How did your brotha take it?"

"He thinks I'm just a kid and that I could never understand him but I do. He's using this trip we're on right now as an excuse."

"An excuse for what?"

"To go find her."

"Oh, that makes sense. Your brotha is like an egg ha-ha."

"Ha-ha why an egg?"

"He tries to be all hard on the outside but deep down he's yellow."

"Ha-ha that's my brother!

"That's a good one," said Peng's voice from nowhere. "Maybe you should tell him that one when he gets here."

Manny and Karina surprisingly turn to the doorway. They see Peng at the door along with a familiar face.

"Mr. Peng!" Manny shouts.

"And you're that guy from the Burger Stan!" Karina adds. "What are you two doin here without the kid's brotha?"

"Darrel is on his way. He got a little caught up."

"Oh, well if you guys aint in a hurry, you can stay for some stew if ya want. I know my show earlier kept you from gettin any food."

Peng looked down at Manny.

"I'm pretty sure it's not poisoned ha-ha," Manny said.

"Ha well in that case don't mind if I do!"

"You aint mad or nothin?" Karina asked.

"No, but when Darrel gets here he's going to be. So let's just relax until he gets here. And don't worry; I'll take care of directing him here."

Ken mixed into the dialogue.

"Well I've got to go," said Ken.

"What? Why?"

"I have some business to take care of. But I got what I needed here. See you around."

Ken exits without another word.

"That guy is weird," Manny points out.

The others laugh. Meanwhile the fray between Darrel and Kyle carries on.

"Allow me to show you what a real chaser can do Dustin!"

The heavy rain has accumulated masses of water everywhere. The liquid is to their ankles and overflowing off the edge of the building. Independent patches of water begin to assemble and slowly mold into solid figures. With each figure being unique, it's hard for Darrel to recognize what is forming.

"What are they?"

"They are my people."

"What are you talking about now?"

"After the massacre, my dreams were filled with the faces of those who were killed by him. Now they will do combat for me."

Darrel starts to see the bodies form. There are not only men, but women and children too. An entire town is reborn before his very eyes.

"NOW ATTACK!"

The remakes cave in on Darrel without hesitation. Two of them grab his arms while a muscular figure begins bombarding him with heavy punches.

Darrel endures a number of attacks until finally he breaks free of the hold. After gaining some distance apart from the clones he takes a second to catch his breath.

"DON'T STOP. KEEP ATTACKING!" Kyle yells.

The clones rush in again. Darrel quickly raises his palm toward the herd of liquid copies.

"THOUSAND HOWLS!" he yells!

His signature black hounds from Maerdym are released from his palm. More and more they pour out of his hand, ravaging the clones all at once. The clones fall again to their liquid forms when they are taken down. As the hounds erase the clones, they themselves also disappear, creating a canceling out effect.

Both Darrel and Kyle are breathing hard. They stare at each other with no intent of backing down, standing alone once again.

"You know, you're pretty good Dustin."

"Thanks, likewise."

"Let's finish this."

"Took the words right out of my mouth."

The scene is all of a sudden interrupted! A massive explosion swallows both chasers whole!

Chapter 8: Max Stein Makes His Appearance

In a dramatic demolition the entire upper half of the building collapses. The top floors cave into the lower half of the small abandoned building. Darrel and Kyle slip into free fall as the ground beneath them disintegrates. The streets are thrown into panic while the fight between the chasers is surrounded by a tremendous cloud of dust. Pieces of the building are scattered everywhere Darrel and Kyle are covered in the debris.

Darrel struggles to pull himself out of the rubble. He diligently searches for the culprit behind the explosion.

"What just happened?!" he shouts at nobody. "Was it Kyle? No he was caught in the blast just like me. He wouldn't take us both out like that. Or would he?"

Darrel's search narrows to finding his golden haired adversary.

"Where could he have gone?"

He then spots Kyle rising to his feet after barely surviving the blast.

"What are you crazy?!" he yells at Kyle. "What did you do?"

Kyle tries his best to shake off the blast. "Don't give me that! I was just about to ask you the same thing!"

"Why would I blow up the building?"

"I've been asking myself the same question!"

"Don't try to change this around! You know it was you!"

"What's your problem?!"

"Gentlemen, gentlemen. Let's not point fingers. After all, I am the one responsible here.

A new being has stepped onto the battlefield. His jeans are ripped and he has a classic cowboy look to him, minus the hat. His dirty blonde hair is long and slips into his face, which at times hides his devilish eyes. This man stands in between Darrel and Kyle with a casual stance, as though he were welcome to the party.

"Kyle, do you know this guy?" Darrel asks.

"It's… him!"

"What are you talking…? Wait, you don't mean-"

"-IT'S MAX STEIN!"

"Ah so you do remember me little Kyle."

"How could I forget you despicable dirty bastard! You murdered some of my closest friends!"

"And now you've led me here to an ideal situation."

"Led? What is he talking about Kyle?"

"How should I know?"

"Same little Kyle. You were always so naïve. Don't you realize what this means? I have a job to do, and that job consists of killing all of you traitors. And at the same time..." Max Stein turns his view toward Darrel. "I see you're sporting that red vest well boy."

"I expected him to notice. If he really is Max Stein, he's sure to know about Xavier's Vest," Darrel thought to himself.

"Yes and those eyes, you are with a doubt of the Dustin family. You don't know how long I've waited for this moment."

"Actually I do have some idea how long. I know all about your hatred for my family. But that doesn't matter to me at all. If that's the case, than you'll just have to take that with you to your grave."

"Rethink this Dustin! This guy is way out of both of our league!"

"You may be a wimp Kyle but I stand up for what I believe in! And I won't let this coward lay a hand on my brother!"

"Coward am I?" said Stein as he raised his arched eyebrow.

"You heard me! Only a coward would bottle a deep hate for an entire family for years, only to take it out on his own people!"

"Don't speak on matters you know nothing about boy! When I returned from losing my comrades to the bloody hands of the Dustin, my so called people turned their backs on me!"

"That's not true Max and you know it!" Kyle yells.

"Well it doesn't matter now because after I kill you two I won't stop there! I'll kill each and every Dustin! Along with you traitors!"

Darrel stepped forward.

"Than I guess there's no reason to talk anymore is there?"

"Dustin, think about this!" Kyle warned.

"What's there to think about? This is all simple to me. He wants us dead, we want him dead. Only one of us can get what we want."

"His attitude's changing," Kyle thought to himself. "When he was fighting me before he seemed more lenient. But now his seriousness is at a new level. But I have to make him realize that he's still no match for Max!"

"Alright let's do it Stein," said Darrel.

"Well at least one of you has the spine to stand up to me."

"DOWNPOUR!" Kyle yelled at the top of his lungs!

Clouds of moisture start to quickly form above. The rain returned, only this time even more fierce. Millions of drops pummeled the ground. It started becoming more and more difficult to see. Darrel made futile attempts to navigate through the rain but instead he felt a hand grab his forearm.

"C'mon this is our chance to escape!"

"Hey let go! What are you doing?"

Kyle pulled Darrel farther and farther away from the blinded Max Stein.

"We don't have time to argue! We've got to get out of here!"

Max Stein didn't bother looking for the two. "This isn't over Dustin!" he yelled. "And Kyle, you can tell the rest of the town that I'm coming for them!"

Kyle and Darrel fled the scene with the echoes of Stein's voice behind them. They ran as fast as they could till they found a safe place to hide. In the middle of a couple of ragged apartments they associated.

"Let go of me!" Darrel said as he snatched his arm away from Kyle.

"Don't be stupid. I'm saving you."

"Give me one reason you would want to save me."

"Because you're strong. And I know if we worked together we could maybe beat Max Stein."

"So why did we run away?"

"Neither of us is at full strength. Not only are we weakened from our fight earlier, but you haven't eaten at all. Tell me I'm wrong!"

"… So what are we supposed to do from here?"

"We've got to regroup. We'll split up and look for anyone who can help. You find your brother and meet me at the Industrial Falls."

"What, why there? It's nothing but a sewage dump."

"The people of New Rialto have formed a resistance. That's where they'll be. Just go there and wait in front of the falls for exactly three minutes and six seconds, no more, no less. Then turn around and the falls will open."

"That's the dumbest-"

"DARREL." Darrel hears a voice.

"What? Who was that?" Darrel asked.

"What are you talking about? Who was what?" Kyle replied.

"Didn't you just hear a voice right now?

"Nope, can't say that I did," Kyle says while giving Darrel a look like he's crazy.

"You're the only one that can hear me Darrel; I'm speaking to you telepathically," the voice continues. "Oh by the way this is Peng."

"Peng? Since when can you speak telepathically?"

"Never mind that. You need directions to our location. From where we parted go east until you reach a small lake. We are in the shack on the edge of the lake."

"Alright got it, I'll be there soon. Where is Manny?"

"He's here doing well."

"Okay good. Tell him I'm coming."

"Will do."

"Who are you talking to weirdo?!"

"Who you calling weirdo blondie?! Anyways that was Peng. He's got my brother so if our business here is done I'm going to jet."

"Don't let him find you Dustin. If you get killed before I have a chance to do it I'll never forgive you."

"Oh shut up. You just better start considering dying that hair. He could probably spot you from a mile away."

"Yeah, whatever. Till we meet again."

Kyle turns and runs into the distance. In a flash Kyle is out of sight.

"Alright time to go deal with this other situation."

Darrel takes off. He sprints through alleys and under shadows trying to avoid being spotted by Max Stein. He finally makes it to Karina's home. The area is quiet but he can hear voices from inside. Darrel takes one last look around to make sure he wasn't followed. Without thinking he bursts into the house!

Chapter 9: Darrel Returns

"Doggie!" Manny shouted.

"Monkey!" Darrel returned.

"What took you Darrel?" Peng asks.

"Sorry, I ran into more trouble than I expected."

"Well still, it's the middle of the afternoon," Karina said as she walked into the room

Darrel's expression changed instantly. He went from overjoyed from seeing his brother safe to burning with revenge toward Karina.

"You've got some nerve. I'm going to give you about three seconds of a head start, before I tear you apart," said Darrel as he stood posted with anger.

Manny and Peng tried to intervene.

"No Doggie wait!"

"It's more to it Darrel, try to be understanding."

"She's not bad Doggie! Honest!"

Their words raced straight through his head like a sports car through an overhead tunnel.

"Get out of the way Manny. I'm going to make her pay for kidnapping you!"

"No Doggie she saved me!"

Darrel stopped. "What?"

Karina spoke once more. "It's Darrel right? Sit down, the stew is almost ready."

Darrel stood in an awkward confusion.

"Go ahead and sit down my boy," Peng suggested.

"Wait a minute, who are you?" Darrel was the only one in the room who hadn't seen Peng's new body.

"Ah yes! I suppose I should revert to a form you are more familiar with."

Peng began glowing with Maerdym light yet again. His dark skin lightened and his appearance shaped shifted into Peng's Caucasian form.

"How many of those things do you have?!" Darrel asked in shock.

"Each of my bodies has a specific role. That form allowed me to speak with you through mind communication."

"Well I guess that answers a couple of my questions."

"Darrel, there is more to this girl than you may think."

"Did she really save you Monkey?"

"Yeah she pulled me out of the fire."

"Humph."

"Okay here it is."

Karina returned from the kitchen with bowls of hot stew in both hands.

"There's enough to go around so don't be shy."

"It looks good, thank you Karina!" Manny shouted as he snatched the a bowl from her hand. He immediately devoured the stew spoon by spoon.

"Kid sure has an appetite. What are you just gonna stand there lookin goofy? Go ahead and dig in."

"Oh, uh, yeah, okay," Darrel couldn't deny the fact that he hadn't eaten all day.

"Well I'm gonna go get some fresh air. You guys can leave whenever. Just leave the bowls on the table."

Karina stepped out of the front door before anyone could reply.

The sun was making its trip down the sky. A breeze swept the tall grasses outside of Karina's home making it look a lot similar to the lake. There were very little sounds this far away from the busy part of town. Karina sat in a patch of grass that wasn't as long as the rest. She could see a group of people walking on the other side of the lake. They all had bags with them as though they were migrating somewhere.

"Hurry along Tania, we are almost there," Karina heard from across the lake.

Soon the herders were out of sight.

"Mind if I join you?"

Darrel had made his way to where Karina was resting on the grass.

"Sure why not?"

He sat down in a bit thicker part of the grass as to keep her personal space intact.

"You look like crap," Karina opened.

"Ha uh yeah, turns out that kid back at the Burger Stan was a chaser too. It's a long story Ha-ha."

"I bet."

"I owe you an apology for before. You saved my brother, I mean even though the fire was your fault in the first place."

"Wow, you really suck at apologies don't ya?"

Darrel recollected his approach. "Look, Manny told me about your family. I'm sorry about what happened. I lost all of my family too. Manny is all I've got. I can't begin to imagine what I'd do if I lost him."

"What happened to your folks?" Karina wondered.

"My mother died soon after Manny was born. And my father was killed in battle."

"Your pops fought in the war too?"

"Yeah, he was a part of the U.S. army. For a while that's where I thought my life would eventually guide me. But, things started changing. My family was taken from me and I was left to look after my little brother by myself."

"Well you're doing okay."

"Ha thanks."

"I gotta question for ya."

"What's up?"

"Who is Erica?"

The breeze strengthened.

"Wh… Who told you about her?"

"Manny was sayin somethin like there were three of you at one time. What happened to her?"

Darrel took a moment to gather his thoughts.

"She left, that's all there is to it."

"There's got to be more than that."

"There's not. You're right there were three of us, but she decided to leave so she left. End of story."

"Did you try to stop her?"

"I… tried, but she wanted to leave. There was nothing I could do."

"But why did she leave?"

"Look that's enough questions okay!"

Darrel quickly turned at the sound of an intruder.

"What are you two doing here? Were you eavesdropping?"

Manny and Peng poked out of the bushes after being caught.

"My apologies Darrel, but we couldn't resist. It's nice to see you two getting along."

"Okay enough. So Karina."

"Yeah?"

"You should consider getting out of this place. They're going to charge you with burning down the restaurant. They'll try and blame the explosion on you too."

"Explosion?"

"It's a long story."

"Karina, I think what Darrel is trying to say is that maybe you should join us on our quest."

"When did I say that?"

"Darrel!"

"But I will admit, it would be helpful to have you along. Let me guess, you lived in New York when you came to America right?"

"Yeah how did you know?"

"I could tell by your accent."

"I had to pick up English quick from those around me."

"And that also means that you should be familiar with the east coast. Well seeing as how that's where we're headed, having you with us would do us good."

"So does that mean she gets to stay?!" Manny exclaimed.

"Only if she wants to..."

The group's attention turned to Karina.

"Well I guess since the kid wants me to, besides there aint much goin on around here anyway."

"Ah, so it's settled. From now on we travel together," said Peng. "Hmm now all we need is a group name."

"NO GROUP NAMES!" Darrel and Karina shouted simultaneously.

Manny smiled upon his new partners.

"Maybe, I can have a family after all." he whispered.

"You say something Monkey?"

"Oh no nothing!"

"No, I'm okay."

"Don't be stubborn now. You haven't slept all night. Get some rest."

"I'm fine Doggie! Really!"

"Why don't you just leave the kid alone? If he said he aint tired than he aint tired!"

"NO BODY ASKED YOU KARINA!"

"WHO ARE YOU YELLIN AT?!"

"Shhh," Peng interrupted. "Look."

They both looked down at Manny. There wasn't a peep out of him. He lay belly down in the soft grass. He was sound asleep...

Chapter 10: Industrial Falls

"It's so hot Doggie," Manny complained.

"Yeah it is getting pretty warm."

"It's because we've left California," Peng informed. "We've been walking for a while now; we should be half way through Arizona."

"Arizona?" Darrel asked.

"Is something wrong?"

"No, it's just that me and that Kyle guy were supposed to meet around here somewhere. Where did he say again?"

"How are we supposed to know dunce?" Karina insulted.

"That mouth is gonna have to go Karina!"

"Oh yeah? And who exactly is gonna make it go huh?"

"Doggie I can walk now," Manny interrupted.

"You just woke up Monkey. Besides this heat could make you dizzy."

"Ugh, Doggie."

"Huh? Oh okay fine have it your way."

"Darrel, it's vital that you remember where to meet with Kyle."

"What? Why? Aren't we supposed to be heading east? We don't have time for detours right?"

"But what about Max Stein?" Peng added.

Darrel paused before answering.

"Forget about Stein. I don't care about him anymore. As long as we head east, he poses no threat to Manny."

"But Doggie, what about all those people he's killing?"

"The kid's right, we can't just leave without handlin our business here first."

"Darrel, there's even more to it than that. You know what I mean..."

Karina and Manny walked silently, feeling they were being left out of the conversation somehow.

"Don't say another word Peng. I'm warning you."

"Darrel, I am trying to say is that Max Stein is dangerous but he is not the only one working with… uh, Folgers…"

"Folgers?"

"Yes… Folgers," Peng repeated while giving Darrel a wink. "You know, the company you used to work for…"

"…Oh yeah. Uh Folgers right. It doesn't matter. I'm done with, Folgers"

"You used to make coffee Doggie?"

"Uh, yeah. But it was only for a little bit."

"How glamorous," Karina said sarcastically.

"That mouth… Wait, I remember now! Industrial Falls. That's not too far from here right?"

"Yes, in fact that is on the route we are on," Peng answered.

"Then what are you hoockos waitin for?!" Karina screamed. "Let's get a move on!"

Karina sped up and raced ahead of the rest of the group.

"Wait for me Karina!" Manny said as he followed.

"Slow down Monkey don't trip!" Darrel yelled as he fell in line.

"Ah to be so young and full energy," Peng thought out loud. "But I myself wish the Wars hadn't messed up gasoline productivity. That way we could drive instead. Oh well, perhaps this boy can bring life back to the way it once was. Perhaps…"

The four traveled through the state of Arizona with haste, stopping only when necessary. The land around them was deserted. People and vegetation were both very scarce and the scorching sun further tested their will to continue. A small convenience store on the road was like an oasis to them, but there wouldn't be another for miles. Their legs begged for a break but their minds persisted in moving forward. The environment they walked on saw a glimpse of hydration in a small puddle of dirty water. And then another, and another. Soon there was a larger pond of sewage water leading up to an enormous broken pipe above head. Sewage ran out of the pipe into the pond like an auburn cascade.

"This is the place," said Darrel.

"Ew, this is nasty Doggie," Manny remarked at the bubbling swamp.

"I gotta agree with the kid. Why did Kyle wanna meet hear?"

"He said that this is where New Rialto's resistance is. So apparently this is where they're hiding."

"Makes sense, I'd never come around this dump even if my worst enemy lived here."

"Hmm."

"What is it Peng?"

"You say the resistance is here, so shouldn't we have seen them by now? Where is everyone?"

"Oh that reminds me! Kyle said there is a special way to get in. Okay he said something about walking up to the falls and turning around. Or something like that..."

"Oh great, Kyle gave information to a guy with the memory of a new born," Karina commented.

"Shut up already. I remember, he said walk up to the falls and wait for... uh... three minutes... and six seconds. Yeah that was it."

"Okay hot shot go ahead and do it then."

"How am I supposed to stand in front of it when it's surrounded by water?"

"How am I supposed to know?"

"I wasn't asking you! Guys any ideas?"

"Maybe you have to hold your breath Doggie," Manny suggested.

"For three minutes? Yeah don't count on it."

"Hmm," Peng hummed.

"That's all you've been saying all day Peng. Just spit it out, we could use all the ideas you got right now."

Peng silently walked to the edge of the swamp. He emitted a deep focus on the bubbling water. Without warning, Peng pressed the palms of his hands together.

"Mr. Peng are you okay?" Manny shouted.

"Monkey, watch, he's changing again."

Darrel, Manny, and Karina watched in awe as Peng's body was blinded by Maerdym light. His clothes remained unchanged, but his appearance underwent a dramatic transformation. His skin got a bit darker, there was a small dark spot in the middle of his forehead, and his hands were covered in rings of all colors. The ground beneath this latest version of Peng cracked and breaking through was a glow with a luxurious flare, burning with a heat fueled by lost imagination. The Maerdym light slowly made its way to the middle of the pond. Just then the ground begins to shake.

"Doggie is this an earthquake?!"

"Just keep watching Monkey…"

The tremor seems never ending, but progress is seen, a pillar of land rises out of the swamp water. More land surfaces, making a pathway from Peng's location to a spot directly in front of the tan waterfall.

"Hey sweet he did it!" Karina yelled.

"Wow, so they can all use Maerdym really good," said Manny.

Peng dropped his hands and reverted to his previous form.

"Peng you alright?" Darrel asked in concern.

"Yes, I'm fine. Just not as young as I used to be ha-ha. The rest is up to you Darrel."

"Yeah, got it."

Darrel walked across the platform till he reached the falls.

"Okay I just gotta wait here for three minutes."

"Don't forget the six seconds genius!" Karina shouted.

"Ugh, that mouth! But she's right, Kyle said not to be off by even a second. Wait, how long have I been standing here so far?!"

"You're at a minute Doggie."

"Oh, right."

Peng looked over at Manny.

"Hmm."

"Oh great that again! What's on your mind now Peng?"

"Oh nothing, just concentrate on getting in those falls."

"How am I supposed to concentrate? All I'm doing is standing here! Monkey time?"

"Two minutes and fifty-four seconds."

"Okay good so it should be about time."

"Three, two, now Doggie!"

Darrel quickly turned around. But nothing happened. He stood waiting while the other's anticipation grew.

"What a dud! Nothing!" Karina yelled in disappointment.

"I don't get it. What did we do wrong?" said Darrel.

"I think I may know what happened," said Peng.

"Well spit it out."

"No wait look!" Manny screamed.

Everyone watched as the falls split straight down the middle. The dividing line grew wider until an inner cave could be seen from the outside.

"Does that mean we did it right?"

"Yep, we did it Doggie!"

"Yeah I guess you're right. Well should we go in?"

"That's what we came here for aint it? Now let's get a move on!"

"You guys sure?" Darrel questioned.

"Why is this even an argument? C'mon let's go already!"

"Yeah, okay let's do it. Manny stay close."

The four cautiously ventured into the cave. For a moment they walked in darkness but it was soon illuminated by light bulbs hanging from the ceiling. The deeper they walked the closer they stood together. Their nerves eased as they began to hear voices from up ahead.

"Doggie!"

"Yeah I know. There are people up ahead!"

"But is that a good or bad thing?" Karina asked.

"Oh look who's scared now!" Darrel mocked Karina.

"SHUT UP! I'M NOT SCARED!"

"Quiet you two," Peng ordered. "Look, we're here."

They stopped and took witness to their new surroundings. There were no more voices. People, but no voices. The room was big but there were so many people packed in it didn't matter. The cold silence went perfectly with the dead stares being drawn by all of the new strangers. Or perhaps Darrel's group was the strangers. After all, they are now intruders.

"Someone's broken in!"

"Does anyone recognize them?! They're intruders!"

"We can take them if we all attack at once!"

"Manny get behind me!"

"Here they come!"

Darrel, Karina, Peng, and Manny huddled together as the angry crowd closed in.

"Wait!"

"It's Kyle!"

Kyle has shown himself once more.

"These aren't intruders. I brought them here."

"What?! Why would you bring them here?! What were you thinking?!"

"They are going to help us defeat Max Stein!" Kyle announced.

The crowd was silent, similar to before.

"They are not our enemy! Trust me, you know I would never steer you wrong!"

The silence persisted.

"It's about time you got here."

"You better be lucky we came at all," Darrel responded.

"Don't get cocky Dustin! Anyway, you guys follow me. We can speak more privately in the back."

Kyle led the others deeper into the large room. They walked past all the suspicious stares and whispers. When they finally made it to the back room an uplifted chatter erupted. Kyle closed the curtains behind them. He turned around and was immediately surprised by who he saw.

"Myra, Clark, What are you doing here?"

Standing at a table with a loaf of bread and a cutting knife is an older looking woman with short gray hair and a gentle aura. She is accompanied by a young boy with dark skin and long dreadlocked hair.

"Clark got hungry so we came in here for a before-bed snack. Were we interrupting something?"

"Kyle!" Clark screamed. "Okay Kyle I'm ready!"

"Ready for what?"

"Don't you remember you said you would teach me how to be a chaser? You're the best chaser here so if you train me one day I can be strong too!"

"Now Clark, let's not get in Kyle's way. I'm sure he's a busy man."

"But mom he promised!"

"Clark, I told you I would train you if you gave me a legitimate reason to desire power."

"Oh, yeah, uh because Maerdym is so cool! And if I were strong like you everyone would look up to me too!"

"I'm sorry Clark. You're not ready yet."

"But why not?"

"Clark let's go. Kyle has important matters to deal with."

Myra tugged at Clark's arm while she pulled him out of the room.

"Clark!" Kyle yelled before they exited. "The day you realize why you're not ready, is the day you'll be ready."

Clark and his mother left the room without another word.

"So let's get started. Like I told you before, alone we are powerless against Max. But if we join forces we can win."

Darrel said nothing.

"Hey don't leave me out just because I'm a girl! I got some fight in me too!" said Karina.

Darrel remained quiet.

"My combat skills aren't what they used to be, but I will contribute as much as I am able to," said Peng.

Darrel had yet to say a word.

"We should begin your training Darrel. There's no time to waste," Peng added.

"He's right Dustin. Not everyone made it to industrial falls. In fact there are many out there who know nothing about the resistance. Time is of the essence."

At last Darrel speaks.

"Don't bother wasting your time training me..."

The group grew wide-eyed at Darrel's statement.

"What are you talking about? We can't do this without you!"

"Well you're going to have to find a way. I'm going to say this one time. I am not going to fight Max Stein!"

"WHAT!"

"DARREL PLEASE RECONSIDER."

"YOU COWARD!"

Darrel turned his back to the people who had once trusted him.

"We're leaving Monkey. You'll be safe in the east."

"But, Doggie-"

"-Let's go Manny!"

Manny stumbled to his brother's side with haste.

"Darrel what the hell are you doin!" Karina scolded. "All that so you could just abandon us here?!"

"I got you here. How much further you pursue Stein is up to you. But Manny is my responsibility! Nothing else matters. You wouldn't understand Karina."

Without another word Darrel takes Manny out of the room. He and his brother storm past the crowd outside. The two left Industrial Falls, apart from the others, but always together...

Chapter 11: Departed Souls

The dry sand turned to tall grass as Darrel and Manny journeyed further and further from the New Rialto Resistance. From heat to humidity, snakes to snails, cacti to red woods.

"You hungry Monkey?"

Manny was unresponsive, holding his head as though studying the grass.

"Manny!"

"I'm not hungry."

Darrel felt the uneasy words from his little brother.

"Manny, I-"

"-Where are we?" Manny spoke, cutting off Darrel's sentence.

Darrel looked around wondering if he had an answer to Manny's question.

"To be honest, I'm not sure."

"Maybe you should call Pepper."

"Pepper? What for?" Darrel asked.

"She's a dog right? Her nose can tell us where to go."

Darrel thought to himself. "Hey good idea. Let me call her."

Darrel's position didn't change.

"What's wrong Doggie?"

"Uh, how exactly do I call her?"

"I thought you knew Doggie."

"Hmm. Maybe it's just like summoning the other wolves. Let me try."

Darrel closed his eyes in concentration. The two paused for a brief moment.

"Is it workin?"

"I don't see her so I would have to guess no. But forget about that for now, let's get you some food."

"How can we get food when we don't know where we are?"

"Look over there." Darrel pointed to a small bush a few feet away. "There are berries on that bush. I can pick some for you and they should hold you over for a little while."

Darrel walked over to the bush and began plucking berries off of the small bush.

"I'm not sure which of these berries are good or bad so I'm gonna try one first."

"But if they are bad than you'll get sick!"

"Don't worry about me. Now let's see." Darrel slowly raised a berry to his mouth and just as he was about to take a bite...

"Darrel wait!" said a voice from behind the bush.

"What the heck?" Darrel shouted as he leaped backward. "Who's there?"

From the bushes the owner of the voice revealed herself.

"Pepper!" Manny shouted

"Greetings Manny. And Darrel I wouldn't eat those berries if I were you. I smell poison in their core."

"So you got my call after all."

"See her nose is really good Doggie!"

"I've been meaning to ask, why do you call him Doggie? He is clearly a human. I'm afraid I don't understand."

"We've held these nicknames for each other since forever. He calls me Doggie because it's kind of close to Darrel. I call him Monkey for the same reason."

"Interesting, there's a lot I can learn from the human world."

"Pepper, we need your help getting out of this forest."

"You need my help for much more than that Darrel," Pepper warned as she turned her eyes in every direction. "We are not alone."

"What? Were we followed? Who is it? Can you tell?"

"The odd thing is… I CAN tell. This scent is familiar to you, there for familiar to me. But I myself have never smelled this person. Also this being is not alone."

"How many are there?"

"Two. One you know. The other is a stranger."

"Well I've been meeting a lot of those lately. But to tell you the truth, every since we entered this forest, I've had a strange feeling."

"What kind of feelin Doggie?"

"Like... something, important is near. I know that doesn't make much sense. Up until now I've been ignoring it. But it looks like what I was feeling isn't completely off."

"What are you going to do Darrel?" Pepper asked.

"...Take me to them."

"Doggie?"

"I don't know why, but I have to do this Monkey."

"Okay. Then I'm going with you."

Darrel didn't argue. He knew that without Karina and Peng, he had no one to look after Manny.

"Show me where they are Pepper."

"As you wish, follow me."

Pepper took off, keeping up a pace that Darrel could follow with Manny on his back. They raced through the bushes, over tree stumps, and deeper into a jungle of mystery. Pepper ran with a steady grace, only looking back to make sure Darrel still followed. Darrel's will was invincible. He sprinted at full speed, with determination alone pushing him forward. He didn't know what this feeling was, but it kept him going. Every step he took was closer to something he needed to see. He couldn't fight the urge building from within. The farther Pepper led him, the more anxious he became. He forgot about his injuries, he cared nothing for his fatigue, and Manny's weight on his back was completely ignored. Further and further they ran. Until he can feel it! They are close! Very close! Pushing himself forward he reaches his destination!

Darrel came to an abrupt stop. His eyes focused on something above.

"Do you know them Darrel?" Pepper asked.

Darrel was speechless. Manny climbed off his brothers back. He looked up ward, hoping to see what has Darrel at a loss for words. At last Darrel speaks...

"Y... you... Er... ERICA!"

Chapter 12: Erica and Darrel: Reunited

"Erica... It's... It's you!"

Standing on an elevated tree limb was Erica. She gazed down at Darrel in silence with eyes that could penetrate a wall of steel. Her long black hair swayed in the wind but the rest of her body stood still, smothered by her dark jeans and petite jean jacket. She had silky light brown skin and a slim figure. The somber expression on her face told Darrel she wasn't happy to see him. The person next to her had yet to turn around.

"So, it is you, Darrel. It's been a long time."

"Erica."

"What's the matter? We haven't seen each other in so long and all you can say is my name? Funny, I thought you would have a few more meaningful words to say. Oh well, if we're done here-"

"-ERICA! Don't you dare walk away from me... again!"

"That's more like it. Get what you need off your chest Darrel. That way we can both move on, I'm very busy."

"What the hell is wrong with you Erica?! Why did you leave? What are you doing? And who is this with you?!"

"I don't believe I'm obligated to answer any of those questions."

"What's happened to you Erica? Why... why did you leave? Why did you leave us? Why did you leave me?"

Manny stayed quiet, knowing not to interrupt the conversation at hand.

"You are still naïve Darrel."

"What did you say?"

"If you really want to know why I left, then I'll tell you. If I stayed with the two of you I would never have become as strong as I have. You were holding me back and so I did what I had to do. It's as simple as that."

"But what about all the good times we had? How could you just forget all of that?! HUH?!"

"I am numb to my pleasant memories Darrel. I only think of the pain because it makes me stronger. Being strong is the only thing that matters. Nothing else is important to me. That includes you."

"How the hell can you say that?! After all we've been through! We met each other during the fourth world war and even though our families fought each other, we became friends! We've been together ever since! Doesn't that mean anything to you?!"

"... It means nothing. I no longer desire to be with you Darrel. I won't say it again."

"You've changed Erica. What happened to the Erica I knew? The one that... that told me-"

"-That's enough Darrel! I no longer wish to continue this conversation!"

That's... BULL ERICA!"

"What?"

"This whole time your shots have been aimed at me! But there was another with us remember?! What about Manny? Why not say you don't wanna be with US instead of be with ME? I know why. It's because you want me to hate you! But I could never hate you Erica! And to be honest... that's what scares me the most."

Erica said nothing.

"Is this worm bothering you Erica?"

The person next to her at last makes his appearance. His face is similar to hers but with shorter hair and a more sinister grin.

"It's fine Paul. I'm handling it."

"Than handle it, we don't have time to waste."

"So you found someone huh Erica? I wish you two the best but that still doesn't explain why you left."

"Shut up fool! This is my brother!"

Both Darrel and Manny were shocked.

"Brother? You never told me you had a brother!"

"Well now you know. And hopefully now you realize, this is where I belong."

"Erica… When did he come? Was it that night you got hurt? Erica I swear I left to get you help."

"You… you said you would always protect me."

"I meant every word Erica…"

"Enough!" her brother interrupted. "If you won't end this Erica than I will!"

"No Paul wait!"

"I've waited long enough. No one stands in the way of the Black Star! Especially not some brat who can't get over the past! The Black Star's ideals stand above all!"

"Pepper what's the Black Star?" Manny whispered.

"I'm not exactly sure. But I have seen the dreams of an organization known as the Black Star. Their goals are corrupt and filled with evil."

"But... Erica can't be working with them, can she?"

"Watch your back Darrel!" Pepper yelled at Darrel. "The Black Star has only the dirtiest chasers in it! Stay alert!"

Darrel looked around him.

"My sister has told me of you being a chaser," said Paul as his body loosened up for battle. "Let's see how powerful you are."

Chapter 13: Darrel and Paul Face Off

Suddenly Darrel was surrounded by a trio of creatures so bizarre it took him a second and third look to believe what he was seeing. His eyes shaded green. His red vest showed that he was now prepared for battle.

The first monster attacks! It's a large canine-like creature with bloodlust in its snake eyes. Its body is covered with reptile scales. It leaps forward but its hind legs remain planted. Its torso extends like a coil making the upper half of its body swing like a wrecking ball. Darrel leaped in the air barely dodging the wrecking ball assault. But he was quickly pursued by the next beast, an oversized gorilla with bull horns and rancid breath. It wound back its massive arm before thrusting its fist into Darrel's chest with devastating force. Darrel went flying until finally crashing into the ground!

"Doggie!"

"Manny stay back," Pepper shouted.

Pepper immediately jumped into the action attempting to protect the injured Darrel from the third monster. This demon had incredible speed and looked similar to a long eared tiger with weighted hind legs. The tiger did battle with Pepper at a blinding rate. They countered each other's attack evenly, matching every strike blow for blow. They viciously snapped and chomped at each other with incredible agility. Eventually Pepper's stamina began depleting.

"That's enough Pasan!" Paul ordered. "Regroup, the three of you!"

The three beasts formed together awaiting their masters next command.

"Doggie!" Manny continued to shout. "Doggie are you okay? Answer me!"

"It's pointless boy!" Paul shouted. "No one can withstand a direct blow from Patu! Especially after leaving himself completely vulnerable from Pamon's attack. And that dog doesn't have any more of a chance of surviving than he does. Nothing can keep up with Pasan's speed!"

Erica interrupts, "Paul what have you-"

"-I got rid of our pest sister! What's the problem?" Paul insisted.

"Noth... nothing Paul. I'm sorry."

"Is that all you got Paul?!"

Paul looked down in complete in shock.

"Impossible!"

"What's the matter? Looks like your brother aint so tough Erica!"

Darrel stood with a staggered posture. The blood running down his chest blended well with his red vest. A dark red river of blood ran out of his mouth down his neck and leaked on to both arms. He was covered in a gory bath.

"Darrel you are in no condition to fight!" Pepper yelled.

"Stay out of this Pepper! This is between me and him!"

"Darrel you are going to get yourself killed!"

"I know you're worried Pepper. If I die, you die right? Don't worry that's not going to happen."

"It doesn't work that way Darrel! Humans fade away but their dreams never die. This is about you staying alive!"

"In that case you're making a big deal about nothing! I'm going to beat him!"

"Is that so?" Paul replied.

"Darrel stop being so stubborn and give up!" Erica shouted. "Paul is in another league. He'll kill you!"

"What should you care Erica?!"

"I... I don't!"

"Then shut up! Like I said... I'M GONNA BEAT HIM! THOUSAND HOWLS!"

Darrel's signature wave of black wolves rush from his palm.

"Demolish them Patu!"

The attacks clash! Patu crushes several wolves at a time with a single swing.

"Rid of them Pamon!"

Pamon sweeps multiple wolves away with its wrecking ball attack!

"Pounce Pasan!"

Pasan's lightning speed is too much for the dark hounds to handle!

"Now, let's finish this! What? Where did he go?"

"Behind you!" Darrel whispered! He appears facing Paul's back.

"What how did he-" Erica stuttered. "So he's gotten better too..."

"Darrel's fast!" Pepper murmured.

Darrel jabbed his rapidly summoned lobo dagger into Paul's back! Paul's blood seeped down Darrel's hand.

The scene darkened. Storm clouds flooded the skies in an ominous manner. The rain was light but the thunder roared in like a lion rising from its slumber.

"It's over," Darrel enforced.

"What's over?"

"Don't act tough. You're done."

"Maybe if you had aimed for my heart. You missed your chance."

"Doesn't matter. My blade went all the way through."

"You have no idea what a Rector is capable of."

"What the hell are you talkin about?"

"Allow me to show you."

Darrel catches a flash of Maerdym light in the corner of his eye. Paul wraps his hand around the blade sticking out of his stomach. But his hands weren't bare; they were masked with a pair of glowing black gloves. He pushed Darrel's dagger out of his body.

Paul palmed the wound on his torso with no sense of pain or fear. The blood shimmered off of his shining gloves.

"What... What is he doing?"

Darrel watched in amazement at this miraculous new event. Paul's injury was slowly healing. The stab began vanishing like a puddle evaporating straight from the ground.

"What are you?!"

"I told you Darrel," said Erica. "We are stronger than you could ever imagine."

Erica too wore the black mystery gloves.

"Patu!"

Patu instantly appears from underneath, breaking straight through the limb Darrel, Paul, Erica stood on. Paul and Erica jumped to safety but Darrel wasn't able to escape Patu's grasp.

"AHHH!"

Patu brutally squeezed the life from Darrel's body. His screams stretched across the forest.

"Doggie!" Manny yelled.

Then from out of nowhere, "VIOLET BREATH!"

Without warning, Patu's arm is engulfed in lavender flames! Darrel's motionless body fell to the ground.

"And just who might you be?" asked Erica.

"You hurt my friend, I'm the one that's gonna be askin the questions around here."

Karina stood tall at her new rival. She arrived on the scene to put an end to Darrel's suffering. She had no intention of backing down.

"You don't know what you're getting yourself into," Erica threatened.

"How about you tell me your name before I beat you to a pulp."

"I'm Erica, and you?"

"Erica?! So you're the witch all this crap is about?! I don't even know why Darrel stresses over you. Don't seem worth it to me."

"What did you say?!"

"You heard me!"

"Karina we don't have time for this fight!"

"Mr. Peng!" Manny shouts.

Peng has also arrived on the battlefield.

"What no way! I'm gonna scorch this witch!"

"Call me a witch one more time!"

"WITCH, WITCH, WI-"

"-KARINA DARREL IS DYING!" Peng shouts.

Everyone paused.

"We have to get him some help immediately. He doesn't have much longer!"

"Peng is right," Pepper adds. "We have to hurry!"

"Yeah… yeah okay you're right. You got lucky this time witch. But next time I'm gonna roast you!"

"What makes any of you think you're getting away?" Paul questions.

"Paul…"

"You still have much more training sister. I see you've yet to rid of your ridiculous emotions."

"I'm sorry Paul," Erika responded with her head down.

"Why the hell do you let him talk to you like that Erica?!"

Darrel's will has given him the strength to stand on his lifeless legs.

"Stay out of matters you don't understand Darrel!" Erica demands.

"I understand completely Erica! You say you've gotten stronger but that's a lie! You've only gotten weaker! So weak that you're letting someone control you now!"

"That's enough out of you boy! I'm going to end your pathetic little life once and for all!" Paul yells.

Before anyone can make a move Peng jumps into action! His body changes revealing yet another new form! This one has tan skin and a full goatee, dark hair, and a round body. Peng's new body begins to inflate until he is about ten times his normal size.

"Mr. Peng what are you doin?"

"Stand back Manny!" Pepper shouts.

Peng then releases all of his gathered air in a powerful gust. The wind is soon followed by a cloud of gray smoke that covers the combat zone.

"Oh I get it!" Karina thinks to herself. "This is our chance to escape! We gotta find Darrel!"

Darrel is now on the ground again. The smoke makes it impossible to see anything more than five feet away. But in the midst of all the chaos a zone of tranquility forms around Darrel. Erica has now entered this zone.

"Er... Erica... why?"

"Stop trying to save me Darrel! Why can't you understand? I want nothing to do with you!"

Darrel responds with silence.

"Just leave me alone. Don't pursue me. Forget about me completely!"

"Is that what you came over here to say?" Darrel says with an emotionless look on his face.

"I don't have much time so I'm going to do this quick."

"What are you doing?"

"I'm healing you. Like I said, I've become a better chaser."

"I don't get you Erica. One minute you want me dead, the next you're healing me."

"I'm repaying a favor okay!"

"…What?"

"You saved my life that night. You know what I mean. The night I left… Now I'm just repaying my dues."

"You don't owe me anything Erica."

"You're right. Not anymore. You're healed."

Darrel examined his body in astonishment. When he looked up, Erica was gone.

"Wait! Erica! Erica!"

"Darrel! Darrel where are ya?!" Darrel hears Karina's voice from afar.

"There ya are! Hop on!"

Karina throws Darrel on top of what appears to be a blimp, but it is actually Peng's body fully inflated again. He flops on and is whisked away. Peng, Karina, Pepper, Manny, and Darrel fly away escaping their near-death experience.

Chapter 14: Rescue

The thunder clouds began to brighten and go their separate ways. Darrel lay unconscious floating in the sky of dark blue. Sweet moisture in the air brushes of his loosely shut eyelashes. At last he awakens.

"Where... Where am I?"

"Where do ya think Einstein?" Darrel hears a familiar voice with a distinct New York flavor.

"What happened? Where's Manny?!"

"I'm right here Doggie."

"Manny! Are you hurt?"

Manny answered with an uncomfortable tone.

"No, I'm okay. Doggie... I'm sorry I couldn't help. I was just too weak."

"Don't be hard on yourself Monkey. I'm just glad you're alright."

"Darrel your actions were reckless," Peng interrupted while carrying the others on his enlarged body. "You could have gotten yourself killed! I'm still baffled at your condition right now. You should be on the brink of death!"

"I too am curious to how your injuries are healed Darrel," says Pepper.

"Yeah, what's goin on?" Karina asks.

Darrel checks his body as though looking for something that wasn't there.

"That's right... It was Erica. She healed me."

"What?! You mean that same witch who was tryin to kill you?! Please tell me this is some sick joke!"

"No. I can't make much sense of it either, but it was definitely her."

"Darrel, this doesn't excuse the fact that you went off alone and put you and Manny in danger."

"Yeah hoocko! Next time give us a head's up before you go runnin off!"

"What?" Darrel replied. "You mean you would have come with me?"

"Of course Darrel," Peng agreed. "We care about you my boy. We care about you as well Manny. We are a team."

"Yeah that's right, even if you do make stupid decisions!"

"You are not alone anymore Darrel," said Pepper.

"Doggie," Manny spoke while tugging on Darrel's jeans. "We have friends now."

Darrel took a moment to absorb his wave of emotions. For the first time in a long time he felt a sense of togetherness. He felt a burden lifted, although he was unsure what that burden was. His dreams had faded long ago, but he now could see a future for himself over the horizon.

"Thank you everyone. Really I mean it. I'm sorry. Please forgive me."

"Consider yourself forgiven my boy."

"And two more things," Darrel added.

"Two?"

"Yeah, first of all... I'm going to kill Max Stein!"

The group paused but didn't seem surprised.

"Really Doggie? Yay!"

"What is your second statement Darrel?"

"I can't beat Stein at my current state. I need to learn what it truly means to be a chaser. Peng, is that offer still valid? Will you teach me?"

Peng thought to himself before answering.

"…Well Darrel, you see it has become a bit more complicated than that."

"What do you mean?"

"You see I specialize in the Gentle Xialon style of chasing. I'm afraid my way would not be beneficial to you now. You see I was raised in an environment where one was not meant to use his power to hurt others. To restrain perhaps, but not to kill. That is a monk's dream."

"So how am I supposed to better understand Maerdym?"

"Well Darrel, if you want to become a better chaser by learning more about Maerdym, why not ask someone who lives in the world herself," said Pepper.

"Could you really teach me Pepper? I've never heard of a human being taught by a dream."

"Just because you have never heard of it, does not make it any less possible. Although, as you know my time here is limited. In order to teach you I will have to take you to the world of dreams itself. I must take you to Maerdym…"

Darrel's shock was written all over his face.

"Really?! I could go to Maerdym?!"

"But of course. Dreams can come to the real world. What makes you think humans can't go to Maerdym?"

"You're kidding! No you're serious! What are we waitin for?! Let's g-"

Darrel stopped himself in the middle of his sentence.

"What is the matter Darrel?" Peng asked.

"Peng. Before we go any further, there's something I need to ask. Something… I need to know…"

"What is it my boy? Speak your mind."

"Doggie?"

"I want you to tell me… about the gloves. The black gloves that both Erica and Paul had. What exactly are they?"

"Well you didn't think the Dustins were the only one of the great families with an heirloom did you?"

"Heirloom?"

"There is a lot to teach, and even more to learn my boy. You see while the Dustins have Xavier's Vest, the Rectors have Sarah's Gloves…

The Time Before part 4: Passing of Dreams

"Save. Save! Save please say something!" Sarah shouted at the top of her lungs. The intensity of the scene made time sit still. There was a spine chilling aura in the air.

"Sarah please! Ha-ha I'm not dead yet, I can hear."

"YET?! Save please don't say that! Oh Save!"

Sarah fell to her knees in an uncontrollable display of tears. She clenched to her bedridden love with all her might.

"Sarah he can't breathe!"

The Saver Piece lies in a hospital bed accompanied by those closest to him, Sarah Rector, Raiyu Nguyen, Xavier Dustin, and Glen Heard. Outside the room was a large crowd waiting on an update of Save's condition.

The time of the third world war had passed due to the efforts of the Saver Piece, and his abilities were now known worldwide. He was recognized as the man who changed the world. But no matter how great he was, he was still human. His life was coming to an end. With details of his illness unknown, the world had no choice but to sit and watch as their savior passed into the next life.

"Save, honey please don't leave me. I don't know what I'll do without you!"

"Sarah... Sarah please stop crying. I'm sorry; I don't know what to say. You know I would never leave you if I had my choice. Sarah, it's out of my hands."

"Don't say that you jerk!" Sarah's sorrow begins to convert into blind fury. She falls into the state of tragedy where one has little to no care for their appearance or what they are displaying to others. A level of sadness that can only be reached when a bond of true love is at stake. The others stare down at Sarah with a sympatric gaze. They too feel what she is going through. Save means a lot to all of them but they also realize that with life, comes death. Though Sarah finds it the most difficult to accept his passing.

"What about Maerdym Save?!"

"Maerdym? Sarah what do you mean? Maerdym continues far beyond my going. As long as we dream, Maerdym will grow."

"Oh yeah?! Then why the hell is Maerdym hypocritical huh?! Answer that Save! Why when I dream of you and me together forever, it's completely ignored?! And why although every time I dream of being in your arms until the end of time, you're still laying here... getting ready to leave me? Why Save... why?"

"Sarah..."

The stillness that follows her intense display of emotion is enough to bring a tear to eyes of stone. Save is left without a word to cling onto. The same goes for the others. Save's brown eyes are surrounded by red as he fights back the tears.

"Sarah... I'm sorry. Sarah if I had one last breath, I'd use it to tell you how much I love you. If I had had one last step, I'd step down to one knee and propose to you once more. If I had one last minute on earth, I'd spend fifty-nine seconds making you smile and the final second for one last kiss. Sarah this is why I need you with me here today, so that I may be with you for eternity. Sarah your love is so powerful; you can stop the pain in this world. And Glen, your knowledge leads to the greatest understanding of the world around you. The way you analyze life is amazing. Xavier, brother, I have always admired your sense of control. You stay in charge of every aspect of your life. And Sensei, I strive to be half the man you are. You are the deepest person I know. I owe so much to all of you. That's why I have taken the time to pass my knowledge of Maerdym to you. But the rest is up to you."

"Up to us?" says Glen.

"Save, what can we do?" Xavier adds.

"You each have not only pure, but strong dreams."

"Strong dreams?"

"Yes. I believe that a chaser lives within everyone. But the four of you hold something special..."

Save paused.

"Save..." Sarah grabbed his hand. "Save your grip is loose... Save!"

"I'm going Sarah... I don't have much longer. I must say one more thing."

"What is it brother?"

"You must search your dreams for your deepest desire. One often dreams that of which is in our conscience. But our deepest desire can be found when want and need collide. You must find the key to this desire... I'm counting on you all..."

Save felt life slipping away. He closed his eyes and began his long eternal sleep.

"SAVE! SAVE!"

The Saver Piece was gone but the mark he left on the world was permanent. He was the man with dreams of peace. And he gave these dreams to those who believed in him from the very beginning.

His brother's name was Xavier Dustin. Xavier believed that the only way to bring peace to the world was to dominate it. By being stronger and faster than those around him, he could bring order to Earth. He used Maerdym to search his dreams for strength. Eventually he found what is now known as Xavier's Vest, an artifact that gifted its wielder unmatched strength and speed. The vest was passed down through the dreams of the Dustin family.

Save's love was Sarah Rector. She had a strong desire for eternal life, not only for her, but for those she cared about. She journeyed through Maerdym for immortality, hoping to end fighting forever. She came across the Rector Gloves which were used to heal even the most fatal diseases and injuries. She came to share the gloves only with her family.

During his time as a professor, the Saver Piece met a student named Glen Heard. Glen wished to maximize the capabilities of Maerdym. He saw himself traveling through time itself to alter not only the past, but also the future. A great concentration as a chaser was required to achieve this; in-turn Glen founded the Heard Band. With it, he could leap to different points of time, hoping to make the world better. Although this power was difficult, Glen attempted to teach it to his family.

While Glen controlled time, Raiyu tried to change reality. A chaser is able to materialize their dreams but only to the limit of their own depth. Raiyu wanted to be able to change reality at his will. His ideals were the most dramatic. Though he didn't have much family, the few he had latched onto followed this great teacher in an attempt to gain the power of his Eastern Symbol.

Inheriting the will of the Saver Piece gave birth to a new effort toward world peace. Although mankind had little knowledge of Maerdym, they trusted the four families with the restoration of the world, but man is trusted far too soon and judged when it is far too late.

The four families were a non-united force. They were a team with no huddle, four bricks with no cement holding them together, and like rivers without a dam, their ideas flowed together clashing in an unproductive manner. Eventually, there was a split, each family working individually. Soon families even began teaching Maerdym to those outside of the bloodline. Groups like Kombinajo were hired and trained to increase military power, but there was only one reason for actions such as these, war! Instead of recovering from World War 3, planet earth was about to enter World War 4. The downfall of the four families was on the horizon...

Chapter 15: Clark and Myra

Clark stood anxiously at the bed side of his mother. The normally crowded small room was empty in respects to her illness. Myra's sheets were on the floor along with her blanket and a pair of shoes and socks. Her condition had worsened. The cold wet towel on her forehead was due to her high fever. There were but a few small candles to light the room.

"Clark, Clark what's wrong?"

"You're sick mom. That's what's wrong. I won't be right until you're better."

"Baby I'm fine. Don't go worrying about me."

"Mom don't play like that with me. I'm not a kid anymore."

"You're not a kid but you're still my baby."

"Mom..." Clark needed extra time to gather up his next statement. He looked to the ground, then slowly back to Myra. "I know that you're dying..."

Myra looked from her son to the wall. She feared this fate herself, but tried not to think about it.

"Clark, death is ju-"

"-Just another part of life, yeah I know but... I just never thought this day would come. Mom, please don't die."

Myra smiled at Clark as though something she kept inside of her was now confirmed.

"Clark, do you know what a dream is?"

"A dream? Yeah it's like a story in your head, like when you sleep."

"And where do dreams go when we wake?"

"To Maerdym right?"

"Ha-ha so you halfway understand."

"What? I'm right aren't I?"

Myra relaxed her mind. Her body was weak because of her condition, but she felt Clark needed to hear this.

"It's true that dreams reside in Maerdym. But there is much more to dreams than a story in our sleep. Dreams are what make us human. They inspire our goals, they hold our memories. Years ago, dreams were unexplainable; everything about them was a mystery. Even now, though we know of Maerdym, people still don't know what exactly arouses a dream. Tell me about your dreams Clark."

The question took Clark by surprise. Though his answer came quickly.

"Well, sometimes I have dreams of you and me in a little house with a big yard. We have a big dog with floppy ears, and the sun is always shining. I want that to come true some day but... if you die..."

"You sound sad."

"Of course I'll be sad! Why would you even have to ask that?"

"Because when someone is sad, they usually cry. I have never seen you shed a tear Clark. Even when your father died."

Clark's attitude calmed at this cold realization.

"Mom, you know how I am. I was sad, really I was, but I just couldn't bring myself to cry. I don't know why."

"Were you sad because he died, or sad because you thought you had to be sad?"

"Mom... I... You know I miss him!"

"I know baby, I know."

"What else is there to dreams?"

"Too much for words baby. Have you ever sleepwalked?"

"No, but I know what it is."

"When someone sleepwalks they get as close to Maerdym as possible without actually being there. They enter a state of consciousness that is but a thin layer away from the dream world. Do you ever daydream?"

"Yeah all the time."

"Daydreams are just as powerful as regular dreams, sometimes stronger. But they can only be accessed by special chasers."

"So how does someone become a chaser?"

"Now that I don't know. But I think it may have more to do with needing to be a chaser rather than wanting to be one. Just remember this, those who lose the will to live, break all bonds with reality. Their dreams of not existing make them the most feared chasers of all."

"But... what does that mean?"

"It means... sometimes pain can kill you, but sometimes it can make you invincible."

Myra closed her eyes.

"Mom! Mom!"

"Relax Clark, I'm just resting my eyes."

"Don't scare me like that."

"I'm not going yet son. I'll stay as long as I can."

Chapter 16: Departure

Darrel and Manny made their return to Industrial falls accompanied by Peng and Karina. Pepper followed closely behind Darrel's lead. They made their way to the room where they first met Clark and Myra, ignoring the suspicious stares trailing them all around. At last they see Kyle sitting on an old wooden bench as though he were waiting.

"So you were able to bring them back after all," said Kyle.

Karina responded.

Darrel eyeballed them both with a puzzled look. "Wait you were trying to bring us back?"

Darrel felt a tug on his pants. He dropped his vision to Manny who was pointing at Pepper.

"What's up Pepper?"

"Darrel we don't have much time. Remember I can only stay in this world for so long."

"Oh right, then I guess we better get straight to the point."

"What have you decided on?" asked Kyle.

"I'm gonna help you against Stein, but first I need to become stronger as a chaser. That's why I've decided to go to Maerdym to train with Pepper."

"Go to Maerdym?! I didn't even know that was possible!"

"Well it is, and it's basically our plan."

"Well I'm definitely going with you."

"It's not really up to me. Pepper what's the verdict? Can he come?"

"It matters not, though you should be warned, Maerdym has the capability of driving you insane. You shouldn't go if you have any doubt at all."

Karina jumped in the middle of the conversation grabbing everyone's attention.

"Wait a minute hold up! So you sayin anyone who wants to go can go?"

"Well yes," Pepper replies still startled by her entrance. "But only if you thi-"

"-I'M GOIN!" Karina shouts cutting off Pepper's sentence.

"Well actually there is one condition."

Excitement quickly turns to disappointment as they wait to hear what the prerequisite is.

"What is it Pepper?"

"You must be a chaser. More plainly you must have the ability to open gates to Maerdym yourself in order to step foot in the dream world."

"Well that's no problem I can do that!" Karina yells.

"Yeah you can, but Manny can't," Darrel adds.

"Oh… Oh yeah that's right."

"It's okay Doggie," says Manny. "I'll stay behind."

"But then who would look after you Manny? I'm not gonna leave you here by yourself."

The group ponders at different scenarios that would allow this trip to work. Each wants the transaction to Maerdym to happen but neither one wants to give up the chance to go.

Peng, who has been quiet until now stares deeply at Manny. His eyes are pacing in their sockets while he thinks of something.

"I will watch over Manny," Peng finally calls out.

"What? Peng you sure?"

"Do we really have time to be unsure? I will take care of Manny while you four head to Maerdym."

Darrel gazed deeply into Peng's eyes. He was very protective and trusted hardly anyone with his brother. Peng's answer was very quick and that made Darrel wonder. But Peng had earned his trust by now. He came to the realization that if Peng really did have an incentive for staying behind with Manny, than it must be a legitimate reason.

"Okay Peng. You stay and watch Manny."

"You have my word his safety will be of utmost importance."

"Honestly, by now you don't need to tell me Peng. I know he'll be safe with you."

"Doggie."

"Yeah? What's up Monkey?"

"Bring me back a souvenir," Manny said with a childish smile on his face.

"Ha-ha gotcha. Okay Pepper I think we're ready. How do we go about doing this?"

Pepper took a couple of steps forward before speaking. "Darrel you and I must be in sync. Dream and dreamer, you must open a gate to Maerdym as though you were releasing a dream. From there I will stable the gate long enough for all of us to pass through."

"Okay... Like this?" Darrel said while closing his eyes and focusing.

Before their very eyes a gray portal is opened, gleaming with Maerdym light.

"Yes that's perfect. Now is our chance, everyone walk through!"

Karina is the first to step into the portal. Her body vanishes but it is not alone. Kyle is the next to go.

"Doggie!"

Darrel turns around and smiles at Manny.

"Don't worry Monkey, I'll be back and stronger than ever."

Manny simply nods his head in agreement. The two share one last look as Pepper walks into the gate and closes the portal completely...

Chapter 17: At Last, Welcome to the Dream World

There was no journey, no road, and no long labyrinth. You simply blinked and found yourself there. The land of impossible, the world of the dreams, Maerdym...

A glow with a luxurious flare, burning with a heat fueled by lost imagination. Maerdym light was everywhere. The sky was... well there was no sky. No definite sky at least. In one area you could see a sky as clear as day but a few meters away there would be an endless nothing above. The land looked as though someone had shaken the world up and left it scattered. There could be a volcano sitting next to an arctic wonderland. Though apart from these bizarre occurrences, Maerdym's initial appearance wasn't so different than earth. There were animals, there was water, and there were even trees. Of course some trees shaded from gold to purple but they were trees none the less.

Darrel was the first to speak. "So this is it huh? Maerdym."

"Yes," Pepper responded. This is my home. This is where I went after you created me Darrel."

Darrel, Karina, and Kyle investigated their new surroundings thoroughly. Kyle wandered away from their entry point. He jumped onto a boulder in order to give himself a better view of the place.

"I know this may sound strange, but it feels like my eyes are better somehow," said Kyle. "It's as though I can see further."

"It's the land Kyle," Pepper answered. "Maerdym isn't spherical like earth. It is a flat world there never stops growing. Every second miles of new content are added so one would never be able to explore all of Maerdym."

"So you mean right now this place is still growin?" Karina asked.

"Precisely."

Darrel looked off into the distance. "So what about nightmares? Are they here too?"

Pepper's expression suddenly turned much more serious.

"Nightmares... are different."

"Different? Different how?"

"You may think you know what a nightmare is, but humanities' view on nightmares is almost entirely wrong. When you have a bad dream, you mistakenly label it as a nightmare. But in actuality it was just that, a bad dream. A nightmare is far worse..."

"So where do nightmares live?"

"On the bottom of Maerdym is a parallel world where nightmares reside. It is a lot smaller than Maerdym but a lot more dangerous."

"So if the boogieman aint a nightmare than what is?" Karina asked sarcastically.

"Karina, murder is a nightmare..."

Karina's sarcastic smile quickly turned cold.

"Deceit, world hunger, apocalypse, these are nightmares."

The group went silent. This realization was a hard pill to swallow. They all knew in their hearts the ever growing problems with mankind. Man has become a selfish race, thinking individually instead of focusing on the big picture. As long as they remained segregated, there would be no justice.

Just then four children walk by. There are two dark skinned children, and two light skinned children. A boy and girl for each. They walk together happily holding hands.

"Do you see that?" Pepper asks the group.

"The kids? Yeah," Darrel answers for them all.

"That was the preachers dream. The one you call King."

"You mean as in Martin Luther?!" Darrel answered in a surprised tone of voice.

"Yes, as I told you before dreams never die. As long as the memories of a person stay on earth, their dreams stay in Maerdym. Dreams are special in that even death cannot take them away. Your body may die but your spirit, your love, your dreams live on."

The children frolic into the distance. Darrel watches them for a minute then turns his attention back to Pepper.

"So tell me something Pepper. How would we find our own dreams?"

"Your dreams? Well usually they have their own place in Maerdym like every other dream but since their creator is here, you should be able to find them fairly easily. Search and your conscience will lead you to them."

"What dream you gonna look for Darrel?" Karina asked out of curiosity.

"I'm just gonna do some wandering around for a little bit."

"Don't wander too far Dustin, we came here because we have business to handle," Kyle remarked as his face grew more stern.

"I know. There's just something I wanna check out."

Without another word Darrel ran off. He was obviously determined to see this "something" because he didn't look back once. Darrel ran past many dreams as he hunted for his own dream. Some dreams startled him while a few made him laugh. He knew he was getting close when he noticed an older version of him in cowboy boots and a tall hat singing in a microphone. It was the odd dream he had long ago of himself as a famous country singer. Finally his pace slowed down. He found what he was looking for. Darrel's nerves tingled. Butterflies were throwing a welcome back party in his stomach. Though through all this he didn't blink once. Darrel slowly crept closer to the spotlight of his attention.

"Erica."

"Hi Darrel, you're looking nice today."

Erica stood before Darrel in a long white dress. She held an unfamiliar smile on her face that lit the area around her. Darrel hadn't seen a kind expression on her face in so long he didn't know how to react. He stuttered a few words and tightened his body in a shy fashion. Darrel dropped his vision to the ground and slowly back to Erica's smile. His gaze became deeper. Golden Memories of him and her flashed across his mind like a strip of film. He had nothing planned to say to her. What would it matter? She is a dream. Darrel simply spoke what his heart instructed.

"I... I've missed your smile Erica."

"Missed it? It hasn't gone anywhere. You always make me smile silly, ha-ha."

Darrel fought his hardest to hold back the depression. His heart wanted to tell him that he had her with him. But his mind knew better. He knew she was only a dream. Yet these feelings were far too real. Darrel took this moment to let emotions out that he had been holding in for so long.

"Erica, we were attacked one night. You got hurt. I said I would always protect you, but I let you get hurt. It was that same night you left. Erica, I'm sorry... I'm sorry! Erica I feel like I've failed you. All my life I've had the people closest to me taken away. But this time it was my fault, it was my fault! If I were stronger... Erica, please forgive me."

"What are you talking about? I've always been here. I'll always be here with you Darrel."

Her words brought a tear to Darrel's eye. He quickly wiped away his show of sorrow. He then turned his back to Erica causing her body to vanish. Darrel opened his eyes and looked into the sky. This was his dream, with a starry night sky overhead. Darrel relaxed his mind.

"Hey," said Karina from his side. She had followed him here... also in curiosity.

"Do you normally sneak up on people like this?" Darrel responded as he finished drying his eyes.

"My bad I just..." Karina searched for the words to say. "You really loved her didn't you?"

"I don't wanna talk about it."

"THEN I DON'T WANNA LISTEN! No, wait, look Darrel I know I aint the best at these conversations or whatever but... the way I see it, you deserve better than this. I mean, you're standin here dreaming about her and she just got done trying to kill you. It just don't seem right if ya ask me."

"Uh thanks."

"What? Why you say it like that?"

"Ha-ha it's just that... you're a little better at these conversations than you give yourself credit for."

"Ha-ha thanks."

Darrel and Karina stood for a few moments with no words. There was only the sound of peace in the air.

"Well, I guess we should get back, you got some training to do big guy," Karina said as she gave Darrel a light punch on the shoulder.

Darrel paused before replying.

"Uh yeah. Let's go."

The two walked ahead. But not even a few feet later Darrel stopped. He turned around and took one final look behind him as though taking one last look at the past.

Chapter 18: A New Objective

Manny waited patiently at the entrance of Industrial Falls. He had a fully loaded backpack hanging from his shoulders and clean clothes on his body. After a big breakfast this morning, he shouldn't be hungry for a while now. The sun raised on what looked like was going to be a beautiful day. Peng walked up to Manny from the inside of Industrial Falls.

"Mr. Peng, you're here!"

"Sorry I took so long Manny. I wanted to make sure I was fully prepared for this journey."

"Where are we goin Mr. Peng?"

"Hmm, let's just say we are going somewhere we can become a much better use to everyone else. Did you eat plenty of food?"

"Yes, I had lots of food."

"Good, than we won't need to stop for a while. Well Manny, are you ready?"

"Um yes I think."

Manny wasn't sure of where Peng was taking him, and normally wouldn't follow, but he knew if his brother trusted Peng, than he should do the same.

Peng and Manny began their adventure toward an unknown destination. They left Industrial Falls and wandered into the heart of the desert. They were lucky spring was here, for if they had been venturing here in the summer the heat would be much worse. They drew a crowd of lizards, snakes, and other fascinated animals. A group of vultures circled them from above waiting for them to fall out so their bodies would be easy picking. The two remained strong. On the way they talked about many different issues, partially to help pass the time, but mostly to learn a bit more about each other.

"So have you ever thought about becoming a chaser Manny?"

"Huh? Me, a chaser? Um no but I think it's cool." Manny didn't know how to respond to the question. He never put any thought into the idea of becoming a chaser.

Peng didn't reply to his answer, instead slightly changing the subject. "Your brother cares about you very much Manny. Wouldn't you like to have the ability to protect him like he protects you?"

"Yes of course, but Doggie doesn't let me get involved too much. He thinks I'm gonna get hurt, but I'm a big boy! I can take it!"

"Perhaps, but Darrel is only looking out for you."

"Yeah, I know."

"But at the same time it would make it a lot easier on him if you knew how to look out for yourself. So that is why I have decided to teach you how to use Maerdym."

"WHAT?! REALLY?! Oh thanks a lot Mr. Peng!"

"Manny you have something that is so rare to find in this day and age, innocence. It may be due to your brother's love, but whatever the case, I don't want you to ever lose this purity. In a way, you and I are a lot alike Manny. I was raised in a place where it was considered never acceptable to hurt others. No matter what, my powers are never to be used for causing pain. And you seem like the type of person who would never want to harm others either. That is why I feel you are suitable for the Gentle Xialon style of chasing."

"What is the difference?"

"The Gentle Xialon style is known throughout the land. I'm sure you know by now that I am able to change into many different bodies, with each having a unique power. But do you recognize anything about my different forms?"

"Uh, oh yeah! They're all different races."

"Yes, you got it my boy. We monks believe in equality of all mankind, so in order to fully understand each race; I transform myself to them using Maerdym. Your answer has also assured me of something I thought before. There have been several instances where your true nature has shown. For instance, back when we attempted to enter Industrial Falls. Our count was off from Darrel but you took that in to consideration beforehand. And just now you proved how observing you are by noticing a key element in my transformations. You have the makings of a chaser, and you didn't even realize it."

Manny tried to cover his look of astonishment.

"So, you really think I should be a chaser?"

"In fact I do my boy. So what do you say?"

"I say yes, if you will teach me," Manny answers while switching moods in rapid succession.

"Ah splendid, and just in time too, because we are here.

Manny and Peng have arrived at a desert fortress. Stone pillars stretch high above and skeletons of those unlucky travelers are scattered on the ground. The flat land makes a dip in which the fortress lays in. There are no signs of life in or around the fort.

"Is this where we're gonna stay?"

"Yes, here we won't be interrupted. We have complete solitude, and we will need it."

"It's kind of scary," said Manny as he slowly slid closer to Peng.

"Don't be afraid Manny, I gave my word to your brother that I would keep you safe, and my word I shall keep."

This statement helped comfort Manny, his body relaxed and his breathing ran regularly again.

"Okay, thank you Mr. Peng."

"Now then, shall we get started?"

"Already?"

"Yes, we aren't sure of how much time we have. We don't know how long Pepper will take training Darrel, and we aren't even sure how time works in the dream world. We need to utilize every second we have."

"Oh, yeah you're right. Let's get started. I'm ready when you are."

"Good sit your things down and sit as still as you can. It's time to test your discipline."

Manny slid his backpack straps off each shoulder slowly and dropped his bag on the ground. He walked over to a clear spot in the dirt and sat down patiently while crossing his legs. The sand was hot on his bottom but he did exactly as he was told with no questions. Peng was somewhat surprised to see Manny obey his order the exact way he had told him. He was amazed by how obedient Manny was, especially being raised by just his older brother alone. Peng did the same, first letting his belongings down on the ground, then walking to a position in front of Manny and sitting down in the same manner. This would begin a long waiting period between the two. They sat in those spots for hours yet not once did Peng here a complaint from Manny. Their clothes drenched with sweat and body odor, though after the first couple of hours their noses became used to the stench. After three hours of waiting Peng called for a break of water, then resumed sitting in the heat. At last Peng opened his mouth to speak.

"How do you feel Manny?"

"I'm okay," Manny barely released feeling everything but okay.

"This exercise is to test your mind more than it is to test your body. Manny there will be times when you just want to break down, but you train yourself to see past these moments of hardship. Stay focused and never give in to your human urges."

Manny was quiet for a few seconds, and then at last spoke back to Peng. "Mr. Peng, will Truth really hold all of the answers we wanna know?"

"I don't know Manny. In fact I'm not sure if I want to know the answers. All we can do is wonder, and search, and hope that the prophecy will open our eyes in ways we never thought possible."

"I want to know the answers."

"Oh do you? Why is that?"

"Because, everyday it's like there are more and more questions. I mean we gotta start gettin some answers for some of them or my brain is gonna overload ha-ha."

"Ha-ha yes that would make one want to know a few answers. There are very specific answers I would like to know."

"Like what?"

Peng wondered if he should reveal the information requested. "I left the temple on a routine journey of enlightenment. I expected to return to the smiles of my friends and families welcoming me back from a long trip, but instead I returned to their bodies, with no smiles. All of my people were killed, the temple was smothered in their blood, and the only evidence I had to go off of was a symbol drawn on the wall. It was the picture of a black star."

"A black star? That's the-"

"-Yes, the same organization that Paul fellow works for."

"But Erica wouldn't be a part of a group like that!"

"Well by what I heard this Erica girl is much different than she was before."

"Yeah, she used to be really nice, to me, to my brother, to everybody."

"Well as hard as it may be to understand, people change Manny."

"Is that why you came here to America? Is the Black Star here?"

"Why would I want to look for the Black Star?"

"You want revenge right? Don't you?"

This question struck Peng by surprise, to think such a young boy could hit such a sensitive spot in the heart."

"No Manny, I have ascended past vengeance. This is what I mean by not giving in to your human urges."

Manny didn't know what to say or think. He ended the conversation with silence. Hours rolled by and the sun at last set for the day. The heat was gone and coolness took its place.

"Let's get ready for bed Manny, we will continue in the morning."

"Oh okay," said Manny happy to be getting some rest.

The two rolled out their sleeping bags and piled their sweaty clothes in an area where they couldn't smell them. After dressing in a set of new clothes they both squirmed into their sleeping bags to welcome the night. Under the stars their tired bodies began drifting away. Peng quickly fell asleep and Manny was due to follow...

"Manny! Don't fall asleep yet!"

Manny looked at Peng who was already fast asleep.

"Who... who's there?"

Manny finally found the source of the voice hidden in the shadows.

"Hello Manny, My name is Glen…"

Chapter 19: Control

"Darrel, allow me to introduce you to my friends. They will be the primary teachers in this session," Pepper instructed.

Darrel and the others looked over at the first teacher. A very hairy man with talons, and fangs over biting his bottom lip stood slouching and chewing a stick of wood. His body was covered in thick red fur. His clothing looked as though it came straight out of a paper shredder.

"To my right is Jor, and to my left..."

The next was much bigger than Jor. His size was overwhelming, being not only extremely tall but bulky as well. He wore green biker clothes with chains coming out of every pocket. There was a bandana over his bald head and scratches all over his face.

"...And this is Erdee to my left."

"Are these things dreams too?!" Karina asked.

"Yes of course," Pepper responded.

"Man I knew you were weird Darrel, but havin dreams like this is downright crazy!"

"Hey shut up these can't be my dreams!"

"Correct," Pepper stated. "These are the dreams of other people. I asked them to help us here today. They are the best teachers in all of Maerdym."

"You give us too much credit mate!" Jor speaks. "But of course if our ol' friend Peppa needs our help we're here to give it right Erdee?"

Erdee nodded in agreement.

"I take it the big one isn't much of a talker," said Kyle.

"Aye which one of these blokes is Darrel?" asked Jor as he looked through the three humans.

"That would be me," said Darrel stepping forward.

"Okay mate you ready?"

Darrel hesitated before answering. He looked back at Kyle who was steadily staring at Erdee. He then turned his gaze to Karina. She smiled back at him and gave a thumb up. Darrel nodded and turned forward to face Jor again.

"Yeah, let's do this."

"That's what I like to hear mate! Now let the first trial begin!"

"First trial?"

"Oh I forgot to tell you Darrel. This session will be split into two trials. The first will be mentored by Jor and the second by Erdee."

"Okay mate I hate waitin so let's get this party started already! Everybody step back. Darrel close your eyes!"

Karina and Kyle stepped back as ordered and to their surprise so did Pepper and Erdee. They stood in a circle surrounding Darrel and Jor. Darrel closed his eyes and was immediately forced to open them again due to the feeling of the ground disappearing from underneath him.

"WHAT THE?!" Darrel shouted. "Where am I? Where is everyone?"

Darrel found himself alone floating midair above a pit of bones. Darrel found himself in the middle of empty space. There was nothing to hold on to and nothing to see. With an unknown force holding him up he struggles to grab on to something, but there was nothing to grab. He began to calm as he noticed his body wasn't falling.

"WHAT'S GOIN ON?! PEPPER, JOR!"

"Relax mate!" Darrel heard Jor's voice but he couldn't see him at all.

"Jor, where are you? No forget that where am I?"

"This is my dreamer's realm mate; you have no control over this zone. And speakin of control, that's exactly what the first trial will make stronger, your control."

"Darrel," Pepper's voice appeared after Jor. "You are naturally adapted to using powerful dreams, but power is but one of the four attributes. It is time to improve your control."

"Alright I'm ready when you are."

"HA-HA-HA the bloke actually thinks he's ready! This should be fun!"

Pepper's voice began to sound more depressed as if she felt sad about something. An image of her body reappeared behind Darrel.

"Darrel, this will not be easy, but it is the only way I know of. Please forgive me... I'm sorry."

Darrel's body temperature suddenly began rising at an alarming rate. His pores steamed open and his breath was hot enough to burn his own tongue. Darrel clenched his pounding chest. His breathing grew uncontrollable. The buildup of heat in his heart finally became too much for him to handle. In a flash Darrel's body burst into flames!

The fire smothered his body in an aura of pain. Darrel screamed in agony.

"AHHH! PEPPER!"

Darrel screamed in pain so horrible it made Pepper turn away. She couldn't watch and she wished she could cover her ears. Darrel's screams grew louder by the minute. As time went on he felt himself going crazy. The torture he was being put through was too much. Darrel pulled at his hair and flailed around in a desperate attempt to relieve the pain but nothing helped.

"Darrel you must control yourself!" Pepper shouted. "The pain isn't real Darrel! Control yourself!"

Darrel couldn't hear Pepper's voice through the screech of his own cries.

"AHHH! PEPPER TURN IT OFF!" he yelled. His cries reached the heart of Pepper. She watched as her dreamer struggled in the ball of fire.

"Darrel..." she spoke in sorrow. "Jor that's enough! Stop the trial!"

"No wait Peppa, give him a little longa mate..."

Darrel felt the flames devouring his body. He floated in the air helplessly burning in his own mind. He felt his skin melting away, but when he looked down it was perfectly intact. He suffered from his fingernails disintegrating but when he checked, they were still there.

"What, what the hell is goin on?!"

"Darrel listen to me!"

"I'M LISTENING!"

Surprised by his response, Pepper hurried to give him the information he needed.

"Darrel you must control your emotions! Imagine that the flames aren't real! You must know the true meaning of insanity!"

"HOW AM I SUPPOSE TO KNOW THE TRUE MEANING OF INSANITY?! I'M ON FIRE!"

"Then why aren't you burning?! Darrel this trial CAN kill you but only if you allow it to!"

Darrel's body calmed for a few brief seconds as he analyzed the situation. He could feel the pain, yet his body showed no damage.

"Think Darrel!" he thought to himself. "Clear your mind. What does she mean by the true meaning of insanity? If you're insane you're insane, that's all there is to it. What else is there? Damn! Why isn't this working? If you're crazy you're insane... or is there more to it? Maybe, insanity isn't real at all. When you dream you express what you desire in life, or in death. So being insane would mean having dreams of insanity. If that's the case than it's wrong to label someone as insane. They are just like everyone else, just with different dreams!

"What's your answer mate?"

Darrel relaxed his body to the best of his ability.

"Darrel," Pepper asked. "What is insanity?"

Darrel turned around to face Pepper's image. "There is no such thing as insanity. Every person is a reflection of their own will; our dreams decide everything we do."

"... By Pete he's got it mate!"

"Now Darrel, release the flames!"

Darrel focused as hard as he could. The pain slowly began to fade away. He stared intensely at his hands as the embers disappeared.

"You did it mate."

Darrel blinked once more and found himself back in the middle of the circle with his friends and dreams.

"Darrel you're back!" Karina exclaimed.

"Yeah, how long have I been gone?"

"About three hours," Kyle answered. "What exactly happened?"

"He made it past the first trial, that's what happened," Jor interrupted.

"Sweet so you did it!"

"Ha-ha wow Karina don't act so surprised."

"I... I aint jerk! I was just... well we were-"

"-We're glad to see you made it back Dustin," Kyle completed.

"Ha you two know these trials can't take me down," Darrel said with a disguising smile on his face. Deep inside his body was still recovering from almost being burned alive.

"Well don't get too cocky mate, now you got the second trial to deal with. My trial is nothin compared to Erdee's. It'll truly make or break you."

Erdee stepped forward without saying a word.

"Do we actually get to watch this one?" Kyle asked.

Darrel looked toward Kyle and Karina with an anxious stare. He didn't want them to see him in the kind of pain he had undergone.

"The next trial will be viewable to all of us," Pepper enlightened. "Now without further delay, Erdee shall we begin?

Erdee nodded in agreement, the second trial was about to begin.

Back on earth an old threat was resurfacing...

"Please Stein, I don't know anything!"

"You're lying to me. I don't like when people lie to me."

Out of the shadows of a dark alley Max Stein had a poor soul cornered with nowhere to run.

"Tell me what you know, or die."

"Okay fine I'll tell you! Just don't hurt me! There's a resistance! I heard about it from an old friend. I don't know where it is but he does! He's been staying in the sewers under Corona's town square! That's all I know Stein I swear!"

Stein turned his back to the cowardly man. He began walking away from the stool pigeon and out of the alley. The man drops his frightened state in a false sense of security.

"Is… Is he letting me live? Oh thank you Stein. Thank-"

BOOM!

An explosion destroys the alley and everything in it!

Chapter 20:
Understanding

Erdee pounded the ground with his massive fist. Everyone watched as the plains before them sunk downward into a stadium like bowl. One by one they jumped in to the many rows above the main flat land below. Darrel also jumped onto one of the rows only to be corrected by Pepper.

"Darrel your place is at the bottom of the stadium."

"Oh okay got it," Darrel agreed while making his way to the bottom. He figured his spot would be different than everyone else's. He stepped foot at the base only to be confronted once again by Pepper.

"Now lay down."

"What?!"

"Don't ask questions, just do it!"

"That mutt is getting pretty demanding. Oh well might as well do as she says," Darrel whispered to himself as he laid flat on his back. "Like this?!"

"Yes now extend your limbs!"

Darrel spread out his arms and legs. His position resembled a star lying on the ground.

"Okay, now what?!"

Out of the ground below him five steel chains surface wrapping Darrel around both arms, both legs, and his neck. Another appears to go around his torso and finally a last chain, much bigger than the others pops out of the ground strapping Darrel down across his chest. Darrel yanked and tugged in an attempt to break free but soon realized that his struggles to escape were in vain.

"Pepper what is this?!"

"These are the chains of understanding Darrel. You see being a chaser comes from a need, not a want. Only by understanding what you are fighting for can you release these chains and complete the second trial."

"Can he breathe with that chain across his neck?!" Karina asked, surprisingly in concern.

"Yeah I'm fine Karina. In fact they don't hurt at all. My biggest fear right now is my body getting stiff from staying in this position ha-ha."

"Don't start makin jokes hoocko! Just hurry up and get out of those chains!" she responded.

"Yeah alright," Darrel tried his best to focus his thoughts on what was important to him. "Let's see, what am I fighting for? That's an easy one. My brother!" he shouted.

The chain across his left arm snaps in half! Darrel freely waves his arm around in success.

"Looks like he got one of them," says Kyle.

"Okay one down, six to go. Now, what else am I fighting for?"

"You must think of everything important to you Darrel," Pepper stated.

"The two people who stayed by my side, even when I abandoned them. There's one who has been a big help to me as of now when he didn't have to at all. And the other, I fight with all the time, but deep down I know we always got each other's back. I fight for my friends, Peng and Karina!"

A second chain breaks, this time across his right leg. Karina smiles at Darrel's comments but tries to hide it.

"I fight for those who push me to be stronger. Those who challenge me to be all I can be and more. That's right Kyle, I even fight for you."

Kyle looked on in silence as the chain across Darrel's left leg shatters.

"I fight for my dreams. Through all of this, I've learned that you're only as strong as your dreams allow you to be. It's up to us to change the world."

Both of Darrel's arms and legs are now free.

"What else Darrel?"

"What else? Well I fight for those who can't fight for themselves. All of the people who need my help, that goes for each and every person at Industrial Falls."

"That's it Darrel, you are understanding now."

The chain around Darrel's torso snaps.

"That's all I got. I can't think of anything else that I fight for, any suggestions guys?"

"NO!" Pepper screams. "Assistance is not allowed in this trial Darrel. We can motivate you, but we cannot tell you what to believe."

"What why not?" Darrel asks.

"Darrel I failed to tell you before the trial begun, but those chains are absolutely permanent. They will never release unless you yourself figure out what is needed to escape. Meaning you can essentially stay trapped forever! And if the chains sense you didn't come up with an answer on your own they will not break. If one of us gave you the right answer, you would be stuck there for the rest of your life."

"That's what I meant mate," says Jor. "My trial could be stopped and tried again later but the chains of understanding can't be undone. That's what makes Erdee's trial so dangerous. It's a good thing the bloke doesn't talk or he'd surely be bragging."

Erdee looked at Jor with a serious expression.

The next few hours flew by. Karina and Kyle went from standing in excitement, to sitting in boredom. Karina even dozed off a time or two. Kyle's patience had finally run out and he exploded in anger at Darrel's failure to escape the chains.

"What's the matter with you Dustin?! And here I thought you were strong, but you can't even break out of a few chains! You're pathetic!"

"You wanna switch places with me Blondie?! Let's see how you like being strapped to the ground!"

"I wouldn't like it! That's why I would solve this stupid thing and get out of there! But you obviously enjoy lying on the ground looking as helpless as an infant!"

"Why don't you just shut up?! I'm trying okay!"

"It's despicable to listen to your whining! Just think, what are you fighting for?!"

"I don't know!"

"What can you not do without no matter what?!"

"I don't know!"

"What do you need to protect?! What drives you forward?! WHAT IS IT DUSTIN?!"

"THE WORLD OKAY!"

The chain across Darrel's neck breaks apart.

"No one could do anything without planet earth! That's why everyone needs to stop this stupid meaningless fighting and work together to protect it! I wanna protect everyone in the world! I won't rest until I do!"

The remainder of the chain slide off Darrel's neck. The spectators look on in delight.

"You can calm down now, the chain broke."

Darrel felt around his neck noticing that the chain was indeed gone.

"Just one more chain to go," Karina whispered. "I need to help Darrel through this but I don't wanna get him trapped forever. Plus I don't know if I really wanna say this, but I think I have to."

Karina steps closer to the edge of her row to get as good a look at Darrel as possible. She stared deeply into his eyes in a way she'd never done before.

"Darrel!" she called out.

"Huh? Yeah what is it Karina?"

"Who... who are you here for?"

"That's the whole point of this. That's what I'm trying to find out."

"I mean Maerdym. Who did you come to Maerdym for? Was it for Manny?"

"What are you getting at? Of course it was for Manny! I need the power to protect him!"

"Is that what you tell yourself?"

"Karina what is this all about?"

"Are you here for him? Or are you here for her?"

Darrel was at a loss for words. Without Karina even identifying who she meant, Darrel knew she was talking about Erica. This question hit him the hardest of all. He secretly battled within himself over this very subject since he stepped foot in Maerdym. A sea of emotion whirl pooled in the pit of Darrel's heart. The same mixed passion that haunted him the second he was reunited with Erica. Before he would try his best to ignore these feelings, but it became clear that he would never escape the past. This one simple question made Darrel question every decision he'd ever made. Erica, Manny, Triple Hawk, they all reflected who he was as a person. He wasn't able to protect the one he cared so much about. To this day he still struggled to keep his brother safe and although his morals told him otherwise, he became a murderer.

"What have I accomplished? What have I become? Am I... am I a monster?"

Karina couldn't believe what she had said. She wished she could have taken it back, but also realized he needed to hear it. She watched Darrel as he lied on the ground in an empty daze.

"Darrel... I didn't mean..."

Darrel has yet to respond.

"Darrel... You do everything for others. I know if it came down to savin your brotha you would give your life in a heartbeat. And that's fine but there comes a time when you need to think about yourself too! You put everyone's dreams before your own. Do you even have a dream? Huh Darrel? DO YA?!"

The others were rendered speechless. All they could do was wait for the two to finish. Pepper especially felt the pain Darrel was undergoing. Her connection with him was through the heart.

"And Erica... Well you already know what I think about that. She's forgotten you, it's time you forget about her. Focus on you Darrel."

"Focus on me? How do I do that?"

"Think about other's future, but focus on your own. Who knows, maybe one day that famous country singer thing will work out for ya."

Darrel's cold expression shatters like a fallen iceberg. Through the deletion of his sorrow, a smile breaks through.

"Ha-ha, a country singer huh? Then I guess that makes you and Peng my background singers."

"Ha-ha dream on hoocko, I only sing lead."

Darrel and Karina smile back at each other with a sense of comfort that spreads throughout the entire group.

"Pepper, I understand now. The biggest chain is broken, by fighting for me. I fight for myself."

"Yes, but do you know that yourself?"

Suddenly Darrel hears a cracking sound nearby. The chain across his chest is breaking before his eyes; it shatters into hundreds of pieces!

"Guess that means yeah," says Jor.

Darrel sluggishly rises from his former position. He is quick to stretch his body and loosen some muscles.

"How do you feel Darrel?" Pepper asks.

"To be honest, I don't know how to feel. But I will say this… I'm ready."

On the other side of the dimensional bridge, Max Stein's hunt continues. Deep in the bowels of an underground sewer Stein has yet another victim in interrogation.

"So you say the resistance is in Industrial Falls?"

"Yes! I was headed there myself, but not anymore Max! I'll leave California! I won't come back; you'll never see me again! Just let me live!"

"Lucky for you I hate liars. So if you're wrong, I'll personally hunt you down and make you wish I'd killed you now."

Stein left the man trembling in fear. He exited the sewers and headed toward Industrial Falls…

Chapter 21: Glen the Time Traveler

"Glen? I don't anybody named Glen. Who are you?!" Manny shouted under the midnight sky.

The mystery man repeated himself once more.

"My name is Glen."

His hair was long; running down his back in a bright red ponytail. He stood tall over Manny and sported a small orange fuzz around his chin line. Glen wore clothes unknown to Manny and similar to a robe with leather patches all over it. Manny turned to Peng and shook his body restlessly.

"Mr. Peng! Mr. Peng wake up!"

Peng was unresponsive.

"He's not going to be up for a while Manny. Now just take it easy and hear me out."

"No! My brother told me to never talk to strangers! Especially if they're wearing weird clothes!" Manny took off running in the opposite direction but to his surprise was cut off by Glen.

"How did you do that? Only my brother can move that fast!"

"Your brother? So you mean Darrel is still alive?!"

Glen's question immediately caught Manny's attention.

"What do you mean? Yeah he's alive! Why wouldn't he be?"

"My apologies Manny, I often forget about other's lack of knowledge when I make my time trips."

"Time trips? Lack of knowledge? What are you talkin about Mr. Glen?"

"So do your questions mean you're ready to listen to me now?"

Manny nodded at Glen. He'd been taught to keep running in situations like this, but the kid in him couldn't escape curiosity.

"What happened to my brother?"

"Nothing, yet... but I've seen many different scenarios of the future Manny. I'm sorry but Darrel dies in the majority of them."

Manny's eyes widened in shock. He tried his best to keep breathing.

"No! But how?!"

"In a number of ways, one was being when I mistakenly traveled to Industrial Falls. I thought I would find you two there, but you had left for some reason. By keeping Peng and your other friend Karina there for just a few more minutes, Darrel was killed by Paul of the Black Star."

"You know about all of that? You really are from the future!"

"Actually I'm from the past. I lived on earth decades ago, during the time of the Saver Piece. I was a student of his and the creator of the Heard Band which you see here on my wrist."

Manny looked closely at the blue wrist band Glen wore.

"With this I can travel through time, though I have still yet to master it. I have altered many dimensions in time, but as long as the end result is right then it doesn't matter what it takes to get there."

"So why did you come to me? You should talk to my brother."

"No Manny, it is you who I came here to see. It is you who has the power to change the outcome of the world."

"Me?! But I'm just a kid!"

"Just a kid now, but when I take you with me through time you will decide on the age you feel appropriate."

"Take me through time?! No way Doggie will let me go!"

"Darrel doesn't have much say in the matter right now does he? But don't worry, when I do take you with me I want Darrel present so he can give his consent. In the mean time, take this."

Glen handed Manny sheets of durably thick paper. They were all covered with writing from the top of the pages to the very bottom edges. The sides looked like they were ripped out of something.

"What is this?"

"Consider yourself honored Manny. For what you hold in your hands, are pages from the coveted book of prophecy. These are pages ripped straight from Truth itself."

"What?! This is what we are looking for! Where did you get these? And why are the pages ripped out?"

"I'll start by saying that it was a struggle just to get those few pages. And I'll add by saying those are the only parts of Truth you need to see for now. There is so much to Maerdym that no one knows. Those pages tell of the other pieces of the puzzle."

"The other pieces?"

"Yes, the Saver Piece is but one of the pieces. The other three are the Omni Piece, the Callous Piece, and the Chosen Piece. When one of the pieces dies they are eventually reincarnated. It is our duty to figure out who the pieces of the puzzle are. Only then can we save the world from Extinction Syndromer."

"What's that?"

"All this information is in those pages, but it is the nightmare that almost destroyed us all back in my time. I believe the nightmares are planning another attack in the near future, though by me being here, the future has greatly changed anyway so there is no way of predicting it. Either way, I believe Darrel is the Saver Piece and if he dies now, the next reincarnation won't be matured in time to help us against the nightmares. So you need to do all you can to stay alive Manny, you and Darrel."

"Okay so I'll give my brother these pages when he gets back."

"No, don't give the pages to Darrel until the time is right."

"But how will I know when the time is right?"

Glen pointed to the papers in Manny's hands. "Read the third paragraph on that top page."

Manny skimmed over the first page. "It says: when the sun falls from the sky, the holder of innocence will defy time itself. But what does that mean? How is the sun gonna fall out of the sky and who is the holder of innocence?"

"The holder of innocence is you Manny. And I interpret defying time as traveling through time with me. The rest you will have to figure out yourself. When we leave, those pages of Truth will hopefully give Darrel enough proof to allow you to come with me."

"I wouldn't be so sure about that."

Glen turned his back to Manny. "Have faith in fate. Truth will guide us to where we need to go. Above all remember this, there is no such thing as insanity. Every person is a reflection of their own will; our dreams decide everything we do."

Glen walked away in a dramatic exit.

"Mr. Glen wait! Where are you goin?!" Manny shouted.

In a blinding flash of Maerdym light, Glen disappears without a trace. Manny searches for any remains but finds nothing. He looks over at Peng who is still fast asleep, but this is no ordinary slumber. In the dreams of the old monk, an equally strange ordeal is going on.

Chapter 22: Ken Comes Back

"Where am I? This is no ordinary dream. I feel an unknown presence. Show yourself intruder!"

Peng stands firm on a risen dirt platform. There is only a six foot area of concrete to stand on, past that is a hundred foot drop. Around him are more platforms. These are a lot more active though, moving up and down like a crowd of elevators. There is very little light in his dream, only enough to barely see. Peng tries his best to seek out the dream invader but has no luck. To his surprise, the culprit reveals himself. Ascending from a platform below is a dark man in an even darker long coat. The man wears a pair of strikingly familiar sun glasses and sports a skin bald head. His face is so plain it's hard to know if it's a face at all. He has no scars, no piercings, no wrinkles, nothing, just a face with bright purple eyes.

"Who are you?" Peng questioned.

"Oh you know me Peng. Or should I say, Malcolm," plead the mystifying stranger.

Peng was astounded by this statement. He stepped back in shock, who was this man? How did he know what he knew? Peng quickly collected himself.

"Every person that knew my real name is dead. Explain yourself."

"Not every person Malcolm." The man's platform drifted closer to Peng's.

"Do not call me by that name!"

"You really do insist on keeping your identity a secret don't you? What are you hiding? What does it even matter anymore? Everyone we knew and loved is gone."

"WE?! What do you mean we? Just who are you?!"

"I am… Well perhaps it'd be better for me to show you. What you are about to see is my original form."

The man's body lit up. Similar to Peng's transformation, his body begins to mutate. The area is brightened by Maerdym light. This fresh body was a bit shorter than the previous and had much longer black hair. He was very thin, and looked of Asian descent. His clothes hadn't changed. Stunned by his recognition of the man's new form, Peng confronts him on this strange outcome.

"I… I know you! You were also a member of Maze! You lived at the temple, didn't you?"

"Correct, and like you I go by a different identity now. You know me as Ken."

"Wait, Ken from the Restaurant? Darrel told me you work for Triple Hawk as a recruiter. A Maze monk would never be involved in an organization so dark."

"I needed to use Triple Hawk in order to get closer to the Black Star, my objective is much like yours Malcolm."

"I told you not to call me that!"

"I will agree not to call you by your real name when others are around. Is that okay with you?"

"…Yes, agreed." Peng felt he had no other choice but to agree for now. His questioning continued. "What did you mean by our objectives being the same?"

"Tell me, why are you here in the states? Why did you develop the Gentle Xialon style? Was it really for protection… or for revenge?"

"I don't know what you're talking about…" Peng responded.

"Don't play dumb with me. You may be a monk, but you are still only human. Vengeance is a pleasure you can't ignore. You would love to have the right to avenge your family and friends. That is why you came here in search of the Black Star. That is why you seek Truth. You're human nature cannot deny the pain of loss."

Peng struggled with the realization of Ken's words. These feelings were all too real to him.

"I remember you now... Your name is Trent. I see you go by the name of Ken now. Which do you prefer to be called by?"

"You can do the same as me; while we are alone we will address one another by our real name, just like old times at the temple."

"Fine, but I am curious as to what your plan is. How will affiliating yourself with Triple Hawk bring you closer to the Black Star?"

Ken stepped from his platform onto Peng's. The two were now as close as they've been since Maze.

"Black Star often recruits new members from Triple Hawk. They seek out exceptional assassins and offer them position as Black Star pawns. Basically they take all of Hawk's chasers and use them for their own personal goals."

"I see, so that explains why you were pursuing Karina. You weren't planning on recruiting her at all were you?"

"No, I wanted to protect her from joining Triple Hawk. There is no future for her in the hands of the Black Star."

"Than why didn't you stop Darrel?"

"Darrel is much different and you know it. I had to give him a choice. In the end it appears he made the right decision."

"So you believe the same as I do, that Darrel may be the next Saver Piece?"

Ken looked off into the distance. "I don't know what to believe anymore brother, but I do know that if he is indeed the Saver Piece, then I will do everything in my power to help his cause. I'm sure you feel the same way."

"I do, but like you said, I am only human..."

"I see, so this is killing you inside as well. It is glad to know I'm not alone. As hard as I try to honor my way of the monk, my hatred for the Black Star grows with each passing day." Ken tightens both his fists. "I... I want them dead."

Peng steps to Ken and puts his hand on Ken's shoulder in an attempt to calm him.

"It is okay my brother. Their day will come. Perhaps by following the Saver Piece, we will see our justice served. There are questions I must know though. How did you survive? And where did you go until now?"

Peng lowered his comforting hand as he allowed Ken to speak.

"I have been closer than you think. I too was on a journey of purity when the temple was slain. In fact I returned almost directly after you did. Call it luck or fate, but since then I followed you every day. At first it was difficult keeping myself hidden, but as you developed your Gentle Xialon style, so did I. By using your same training methods I was able to split my body as well. The form you see now is the form I used to keep you from noticing me. I am able to become completely invisible in this body. The one I was in earlier has the ability to enter a person's dreams."

"I don't understand. Why hide from me? With your abilities joined with mine we could have confronted the Black Star directly."

"That is the exact reason brother. Both of our minds are clouded and our decisions would be derived directly of vengeance. We must not allow ourselves to stray down this path. That is why it is best we journey separately, but at the same time we are always together."

"…Yes you're right. Forgive me it's been so long since I've spoken with another from Maze."

"You owe neither me nor anyone else an apology Malcolm. Just stay true to Maze. I will do all I can on the inside, you must guide the Saver Piece. He may be our last hope for survival."

"Yes, I will. Thank you."

"Just to let you know, that boy, Manny has also encountered someone on the outside."

"What who? Is Manny in danger?"

"No quite the opposite. He has been given something very grand. You will come to find out what it is soon. One more thing before I leave…" Ken took a long pause before continuing. "Max Stein is on his way to Industrial Falls."

"What?!"

"Calm yourself brother, it will take him at least two more days to get there. He has a few stops to make first. Just make sure you and the others are ready around that time."

"Where will you go Trent?"

"I don't know brother. Where ever Maerdym takes me. I bid you farewell for now."

Ken walked back onto his platform. He gave Peng a last look before vanishing out of sight.

"I have a feeling we will meet again much sooner than you think Trent, good luck my brother."

With that Peng wakes from his dream. He is blinded by the morning sun and surprised to see Manny up stretching.

"You're up early Manny."

"Mr. Peng… I'm ready to learn. Please teach me all you can."

Peng stared at Manny. He saw new determination in his eyes. What Ken said was true. Though Peng wasn't sure what Manny went through, he was sure this boy was now prepared for the battle ahead.

"Yes my boy, let us continue…"

Chapter 23: Triple Hawk Meeting

"I'm glad you could see me this evening Max. I know you are very busy these days with your seek for revenge and all."

"What is this all about? Why have you called me here?" The notorious Max Stein has arrived at the headquarters of Triple Hawk. He and three others occupy a small room with plenty of papers and other miscellaneous objects flooding the floors. Bounty posters cover the walls so much, there is no need for paint or wallpaper. Stein and the other occupants are set up much like a job interview, with everyone facing Stein. The owner of Triple Hawk is sitting in the middle of his two hired assassins.

"Well you see Max, the situation has changed a bit. Your successful collection of bounties haven't gone unnoticed; in fact you've been recognized by an organization that we affiliate ourselves with. If we have any exceptional employees, they are offered to this organization known as the Black Star."

"I know who the Black Star is."

"Yes well in return for our assassins, we receive a very generous financial reward."

"So what you're telling me is that you want to sell me out, is that right? Thanks but no thanks. I haven't completed my most previous mission."

"Ah yes, the mission to kill the people of New Rialto, don't worry about that, I will see that another one of my men gets on it. Don't pass up this opportunity Max. There are many who would kill to be in your position."

"There are many who would kill for a slice of cheese. Isn't that why they work for you Marshal? Stein stood up out of his seat and headed toward the door. "If you're wondering, I refuse your offer."

"So what I suspected was true," Marshal says, halting Stein's walk.

"What are you blabbing about now?"

Marshal folds his fingers into each other while he speaks. "I did a little investigating Max. It seemed odd that you would be the one to accept this mission to kill the people of New Rialto. You submitted the bounty Max, didn't you?"

"What should it matter to you? You're getting paid and I get my revenge. Everybody wins."

"That's not how we do business here Max. I'm expelling this mission!"

"HA-HA-HA-HA-HA."

Marshal and his men look at each other, then back to Stein.

"I'm sorry, did I say something funny?"

"It just makes me laugh knowing that you posers actually think I care! This mission means nothing to me, I'm going to kill them either way! I tried to let you be the middle man, but now your usefulness has run out, goodbye!"

Stein quickly springs at Marshal and his guards. Before either of them can think, he is directly in Marshal's face shoving something down his throat. This something is an explosive. Without any time to react... *BOOM!*

After an amazing flash, years of work is destroyed in an instant with nothing left but a cold hearted avenger in the dust. The entire Triple Hawk office is now falling from the sky, in a shower of rubble. Amazingly, Stein walks away from the disaster seen with his wounds healing much faster than usual.

"Fools, they didn't realize I had no use for them at all. Now it's time to extract my revenge, at Industrial Falls."

Chapter 24: The Calm

Industrials Falls was as quiet as a roaring falls could be. The silence was terrifying, like a calm before the storm. Peng and Manny returned to the falls, expecting to see Darrel and the others back from Maerdym, but they were nowhere to be found. The monk and young chaser in training hadn't spoke at all about the night with Ken and Glen. The feeling of uncertainty was mutual, Manny was uncertain of telling Peng about Glen, and Peng was uncertain of exactly how much Manny knew.

"Why was it so important for us to get here now Mr. Peng?"

"I just wanted to be back before your brother and Karina returned. We can practice till then."

"Oh, okay." Peng's words couldn't fool Manny, he knew there was more to it than that but he decided not to further the conversation.

"Speaking of practice, let's see what you've learned so far."

"Okay!" Manny responded in an enthusiastic tone.

He ran to the edge of the sewage lake and closed his eyes. Manny put his hands together as if he was praying but in fact he was concentrating on opening his very own Maerdym gate. His hands slowly opened. A small portal formed in between his hands that sparkled with Maerdym light. Suddenly the area explodes around Manny!

"Manny!" Peng calls out. "What happened? What did he summon?"

"He didn't summon anything..." says a voice from nowhere.

Peng hastily turns around to see who has arrived on the scene.

"So, you're here after all... Max Stein!"

At the top of a small hill stands no other than Max Stein. The light from the sun shines on his dark soul. The face of evil has come at last. Though Darrel is nowhere in sight.

"Manny are you okay?!" Peng yells as he rushes to the smoky area where Manny once stood, he frantically searches for Manny in the debris.

"Mr. Peng! I'm over here Mr. Peng!"

Peng pulls Manny out of the dirt and sets him on the ground.

"Manny are you okay?"

"Yeah I'm okay. Who is that guy?"

"That's Max Stein."

"The guy my brother was talkin about?"

"Yes this is him in the flesh. I think it's best if you stay back and let me handle this."

Manny stood frightened and at the same time confident. Peng could see in Manny's eyes the heart of a warrior.

"There is something... different in this boy," he thought to himself. He then faced Stein ready for the battle ahead.

"Are you prepared to die old man?"

"Whatever happens, keep away from this fight Manny. Okay Stein let's get started."

Manny's worry didn't surface until he was forced to watch instead of fight. "Mr. Peng can't fight this guy. His style isn't for killing. I have to help him but..."

"Well let's start by seeing what you've got old timer!"

Stein tosses an explosive toward Peng! Peng has no time to dodge but instantly changes to his Indian form. He creates a pillar from the ground in front of him to block the bomb.

"Not bad old man! But what if I come from above?!"

Stein takes a drastic leap into the air over the stone block made by Peng. He is left defenseless and must think quickly in order to survive the next attack! Peng's next move is a desperate one. He changes form once again into his Hispanic body and immediately inflates to his big body of air.

"What the…?" Stein yells as he bounces right off of Peng's body. After flinging into the air Stein winds his body around delivering a round house kick directly to Peng's face! Peng's body deflates pushing him far away from the point of contact. Stein then follows up with another one of his signature Maerdym hand explosives thrown at Peng as he hits the ground. *BOOM!*

"OH NO! MR. PENG!" Manny screams.

"Don't worry boy! You're next!" Stein yells.

Stein dashes toward Manny with his hand in a throat grasping motion, but as soon as he reaches the boy, a different hand has wrapped around his wrist!

"Hey, no one lays a hand on my brother! Got that?"

At last Darrel has arrived and not a moment too soon! Karina appears behind Manny with Kyle behind her.

"Karina!" Manny shouts with joy. He turns around and gives her the biggest hug his little arms will allow.

"Ha-ha hey kid did ya miss me?"

"Yeah I did!"

"Manny!" Darrel's deep commanding voice calls to his little brother. He releases Stein's wrist and prepares for battle. "How are you doing?"

"I… I'm good Doggie," Manny answers in slight hesitation. He isn't sure what it is, but he senses something different in his big brother and yet only three days have passed.

"Good, now watch as your big brother handles his business."

"Ah yes I remember you. You're the coward who ran away back in Corona. I see you're here as well Kyle."

People from inside of Industrial Falls begin storming out of the cave wondering what all the commotion outside is about. Clark and Myra are not present this herd.

"It's Max Stein!"

"Run for your lives!"

"Oh no he's found us!"

Every one runs around in panic as they look upon their assured deaths ahead. Screams grow louder and chaos brews. Darrel readily takes charge of the situation.

"Everyone calm down! I'm here to save you! I will protect you!"

A few people start to slow down and listen to his words. These few start a chain reaction with others.

"I know you don't know me very well and I know you don't have much trust in me, but I promise you if you stick by my side I will take you out of this nightmare!"

Without further hesitation Kyle steps in to the speech. "Listen to him everyone!" With his voice the remainders of people stop to listen. "But you can't do this alone Dustin!"

"I told you before, this is my fight!"

"This is more my fight than yours idiot! Let me help you!"

"NO!" Darrel's rage transforms him. His eyes glow green and Xavier's Vest covers his chest. "Stay out of it! For once I will keep my word and protect my friends!" Darrel raises his hand to summon the lobo dagger but this time it is a bit larger, looking more like a lobo short sword. "It's time Stein!"

Stein smiles in excitement. "Ha-ha now this is what I'm talking about! Bring it on! I finally get to spill Dustin blood!"

"You're mad Stein, but your madness will be your downfall."

"Enough talk! FIGHT ME!"

Stein flies forward with Maerdym light in his hands. He summons a long curved weapon with a pale color and a handle made of ropes. Darrel also dashes ahead to face off against Stein. With a clash of their weapons, the battle begins!

Chapter 25: The Storm

The chaser dual commenced! Darrel and Stein swung their weapons with all their might, both is intending to overpower the other. The land beneath them cracks under the pressure of their attacks. Shockwaves go flying amongst the people witnessing the fray. Darrel and Stein stare into each other's eyes. These moments bring enemies together even under the harshest conditions. While in combat, rivals peer deeper into each other's soul with every blow. Through every attack they are reminded of why they are enemies in the first place. It is their dreams, their motives conflict with each other causing them to do battle.

Darrel springs back from the next attack, but to his surprise Stein's next move is a long ranged assault!

"Take this!" Stein shouts as he hurls his heavy rapier.

The curled weapon spins rapidly at Darrel!

"Doggie!" Manny yells.

Darrel just barely avoids the attack by ducking under the blade. The fine edge shaves a few hairs off his head. He winds back and prepares for a counter attack but the boomerang sword is whipping around and going for a second attempt at slicing Darrel in half! Darrel turns just in time to block the attack with Lobo Blade. Stein takes this chance to sneak a heavy punch aimed at Darrel's ribs. Darrel hits the ground hard, spitting up blood as he rolled.

"Darrel look out!" Karina screamed!

Stein immediately follows up his last attack with a finishing strike from above! To his surprise Darrel is defended against the attack from a body, but who's body?

"Kyle!" Darrel yelled in shock.

Kyle used one of his summoned bodies to block Stein.

"I told you I'd help. Your welcome."

Darrel stood up. "Thanks. Who was that you sacrificed?"

"…He was my best friend. I didn't have much time to think and he was the first person I thought about. This bastard killed him. You have to win this fight Dustin. You don't have a choice!"

"Yeah, I know. Thanks again, but he's on the move. Take cover."

Darrel was right. Stein wound back his weapon then swung it forward with great strength. A flock of explosives are sent flying Darrel's way. Without hesitation he raises his palm at Stein.

"THOUSAND HOWLS!" Darrel cries as the black Maerdym wolves rush from his hand. The hounds bite and claw Stein's bombs making them each detonate prematurely. The wolves' stay is short but their contribution is much needed. Left behind is a cloud of smoke blinding the combatants' view of each other, though sight isn't required when you have the nose of a blood hound. From the haze leaps one more wolf! It's Pepper! She pounces on the unsuspecting Max Stein ripping a chunk of his shoulder off!

"AHH! YOU DAMNED MUTT!" Stein yells as he swings Pepper off of him.

The smoke clears enabling Darrel to see once again. "Pepper!"

"No time for greetings Darrel! He's coming!"

Max Stein held his bloody shoulder in pain but showed no sense of worry. The people of New Rialto stood anxiously waiting for the resolution of the battle. Children clenched onto parents, parents clenched onto hope. Stein looked up and began laughing in a demonic tone. His face looked truly like a person who had lost his mind. His wound slowly started healing.

"What's going on?!" Darrel asked out loud. "How does he have that power? Is he a Rector too?"

Stein's muscles suddenly increase in size. His veins grow larger and his voice deepens. His evil laugh is even more repulsive now.

"Darrel!" From the rubble, Peng rises. He is scarred and bruised from head to toe. "Listen, Kombinajo worked for both the Rector and Dustin family. Not only that, but they were also trained by the two clans. In a way Stein will have powers similar to Xavier's Vest and the Rector Gloves."

"You're kidding me! So he has super strength, speed, and regeneration? Great!"

"Although his abilities aren't as skilled as an actual member of the family. Don't lose faith! You can beat him!

Without warning Stein instantly darts in front of Darrel. Darrel is caught off guard and doesn't have a chance to react. Max delivers a massive knee thrust into Darrel's already broken ribs! Darrel is then pounded into the dirt by Stein's overwhelming forearm!

The young hero is out cold. Screams of his name echo through the air.

"DARREL NO!" Karina calls out. Her patience runs out and she jumps into action! "VIOLET BREATH!" she screams as she attempts to engulf Stein in her lavender flames! Unfortunately the fire isn't strong enough! Stein rips through the embers and sends Karina flying with a monstrous blow!

"AH-HA-HA-HA! Don't you see? I can't be stopped! Now let's finish this my former townspeople!"

Stein turns to the people of New Rialto who are now tightly packed together. The fear in their face is too obvious, but they stand firm ready to face this menace.

"No!" Kyle yells jumping in between Stein and the crowd. "If you want them, you'll have to get through me! I know you're stronger than me Max, but I won't let my people die without putting up a fight!"

Kyle hastily runs at Stein carrying a fist meant to take the murderer down once and for all. He swings but his attack is proved futile in the palm of Stein's hand. Stein then grips Kyle's fist and brutally bends his wrist downward breaking the bone in Kyle's arm! He drops to his knees holding his left arm and screaming in agony from the pain.

Stein slowly walks past Kyle unfazed by the man's cries at all.

"Now, where were we?" Stein takes one step forward, the people tremble in fear. He takes another step, their bodies tense up. Before Stein takes his third step he notices something or someone at the corner of his eye. His progression stops and he turns to face this new distraction.

"Ah yes, the boy!" Stein's new target is Manny! "I believe we have unfinished business kid. I think I'll handle you first."

Stein uses his speed to appear at Manny's side. Manny stares at him with fear pouring from his pupils. The situation has locked his body. He can't move or speak. Stein raises his foot and demolishes Manny with his boot. The boy was repeatedly stomped into the soil! One after another the trampling continued while Stein fills the area with his sinister laugh.

Stein stomps! Darrel's heart pounds! Stein pounds! Darrel's unconscious body twitches! Stein pummels Manny! DARREL SNAPS!

Chapter 26: Two Minds, One World

       Darrel finds himself drifting in a sapphire abyss. He has escaped reality and now released his mind to a freefall of thought. He is not alone. Max Stein has also entered this realm of tranquility. The two float on parallel waves of emptiness that never end, yet never go anywhere.

       "Where am I?" Darrel thought to himself. Though he never once opened his mouth, his words echoed across the air.

       "How should I know?" Stein replied, also speaking through his mind.

       "What so you can read my mind now too? That doesn't matter. You hurt my brother!"

       "Calm down idiot. We're obviously caught in our own thoughts. I don't know exactly how this happened and I also have no idea how to get back, but if you've noticed, we're both completed immobilized."

       Darrel tried to move his body. He couldn't even make his eyes blink. "But how did you know I couldn't move?"

"I've heard of this. It's called chaser sync. Right now we are in a dimension with no time. It's like a wrinkle in reality."

"This doesn't make sense. Why am I here with you? I HATE YOU!"

"How can you hate something you don't understand? You know nothing about me."

"I know plenty about you Max Stein. You kill the innocent. You're a heartless murderer."

Stein paused. "Do you know what it's like to have everyone you love taken away from you? I'm called a murderer, I'm called heartless, but these words will never change my life's objective. I must avenge Kombinajo."

"How can you call this pointless killing vengeance? You're doing nothing but disgracing your comrade's lives with a cowardly assault on those who can't protect themselves."

"You don't understand blind hatred boy! Those three... they were more than comrades. They were like brothers to me. No, they WERE my brothers. I wouldn't hesitate to give my life for each and every one of them! And I know that they would do the exact same for me. We spent our lives watching each other's backs. No matter what, we were always there for each other. Just by surviving the Dustin's attack and not dying alongside them, I feel I've betrayed them. This sadness quickly developed into a careless malice toward everyone. I use any excuse I can to kill. I just... I just don't care anymore."

Stein's words left Darrel speechless for a moment. "You may not think I do, but I understand your pain Stein," he said in a calmer voice. "When I was ten my mom died. And not too long after that my dad was killed in battle. For a while I thought I'd never get over their deaths. In a way I still haven't."

Stein spoke once more. "Then perhaps you do understand a little. You understand the feelings memories can cause. We had our bad times, but we had some damned good ones too. It hurts worse than any wound knowing I'll never see their smiles again. I never even got to say goodbye." Max Stein's eyes wanted so badly to cry. But his heart had frozen solid a long time ago. There was nothing to cry from, and nothing left to cry for. Instead he swallowed his emotions like he'd done every day of his life.

"It's not too late to say goodbye," Darrel responded, but his statement drew no reply from Stein.

"Tell me, have you heard of the Callous Piece?"

"No can't say that I have."

"He's a being with no emotion. No matter what happens or what he goes through, he never feels a thing. He is much different than the Saver Piece.

Years ago, people admired the Saver Piece for his power and influence. But I myself am more inspired by the Callous Piece. To think, he feels nothing at all. To be callous one must abandoned everything. Their sorrow, their anger, even their happiness, I was able to do neither."

"Well if you ask me, that isn't the way a person should live. I believe people need their emotions, even hatred, just as long as we know how to control our emotions."

"Hatred can never be controlled. It lives within us all, you, me, even your little brother. It's only a matter of time before it surfaces."

Darrel's paralysis broke with a smile. "You don't think I know this? That's exactly why I try everyday to teach him how to use his emotions in productive ways. Hopefully when he gets older, he'll live in a world with peace. No more racism, no more sexism, no more gangs, no more... hate."

Stein too was able to slightly move his body. He turned his head to face Darrel. "We can only dream boy... we can only dream."

With that the two feel their bodies hazing away. They are at last leaving this mysterious plain.

"When we return, it will be like this never happened," said Stein.

"Maybe it's best that way," Darrel replied.

Darrel and Stein return to themselves, and to the battlefield.

Chapter 27: Corona Soul

Darrel erupted in Maerdym light! His limbs were taken by the paladin glow, his mind was unaware of the transformation at hand. Darrel had once again slipped into the dark zone; images of his past and all the things he'd gone through recently floated around in his brain. Losing his mother and father, raising his brother, Erica leaving, seeing her again, meeting Peng and Karina, experiencing near death physically on earth, mentally in Maerdym, taking it in his hands to save an entire city! All these events led him here, the time was now!

Darrel rose from his state of defeat. He raised his eyes to Stein mentally burning him with a flame of passion! Everyone's eyes were on Darrel. He wasn't here to lose, his new motivation was impenetrable!

"Stein!" Darrel called with a thunderous roar in his voice. His green eyes glowed brighter than usual but Lobo Blade was nowhere to be found.

"What are you going to fight me with no weapon? You're even dumber than I thought!" Stein's banter is cut short. He looks into Darrel's eyes and sees something entirely different. He sees a man with no fear. He sees a man with nothing to lose. He sees a man with no concern for his own life.

"You hurt my brother!"

From his neck down, Darrel is shrouded by a glow with a luxurious flare, burning with a heat fueled by lost imagination. This light was familiar to everyone.

"You hurt my friends!"

When the shine fades Darrel's wrists and ankles are wrapped by steel chains. The chains lead all the way upward into the cloudy sky!

`   "I won't forgive you!"

"I didn't ask for your forgiveness!" Stein shouts as he dashes toward Darrel! The assassin prepares to give the final blow, but again something more catches his attention. Stein comes to a halt. He looks in fear at the sky above. What is in the sky?

From Darrel himself, the summoned chains lead into the clouds above. The clouds seem to be hiding something of their own. A golden radiance simmered through the barrier of shade. A source of light hid from the world below, but was soon to reveal itself!

Manny crawled his way to Pepper's side. "Pepper, what is that in the sky?"

"I don't know if he ever told you this, but Darrel has recently dreamed of carrying the sun itself. It may be due to the burdens life has weighed upon him, but either way this is how his dreams have expressed it."

"So you mean that thing up there is..."

Breaking through the clouds now is a peak of intense flames! The fire reveals more and more of itself eventually passing the clouds completely and floating in the space between ground and sky. A diminutive version of the sun has arrived, chained to Darrel's arms and legs!

"It's the sun Stein. If you were wondering what has brought chills down your spine, it is the sun! With this I'll end this once and for all!"

Instead of showing fear Max Stein again lets out a hideous laughter.

"Fool, who do you think you're dealing with?! I watched the people closest to me murdered in cold blood before my very eyes! I have been to hell and back! Do you think a snot nosed brat with a few tricks up his sleeves would scare me?!"

"I have no reason to scare you Stein. I wouldn't waste my time scaring someone who would kill his own people!"

"HA-HA, do you want to hear the truth behind this boy?! The truth is I was the one who submitted the bounty request for the people of New Rialto!"

The crowd grows frantic with disbelief. Their fear quickly turns to hatred. Most of them can't believe what they've heard!

"That's right I said it! I can't stand any of you! You betrayed me when I was down and now I'm going to repay every dime of deceit! There is no longer a middle man; I dealt with Triple Hawk myself!"

Darrel was shocked to hear that Triple Hawk was no more, but at the same time his heart eased just a little bit.

"I've heard enough Stein, let's finish this."

"I couldn't agree more!" Stein again races toward Darrel at full speed! "You can't kill me boy! I am the true face of corruption! You can't even begin to fathom what I've gone through to reach this level of insanity! YOU CAN'T KILL WHAT YOU DON'T UNDERSTAND!"

Darrel closed his eyes for a brief moment. When he reopened them he spoke. "You're wrong Stein. I do understand now. What you've become isn't a result of insanity at all. You are a product of you own dreams."

Darrel pulls on the chains with all his might! Every muscle in his body tenses up. Sweat runs down his face like a leaky faucet. His body is firmly planted in the ground. The tension on the chains pulls the sun toward the earth and over Darrel. Stein and the sun are headed for a collision!

"I WILL NOT DIE!"

"LET'S END THIS STEIN! CORONA SOUL!"

The sun swallows Stein whole! He struggles to keep running toward Darrel but soon loses his footing and drifts into the center! His clothes are scorched away and his hair burns to the root.

"AHHH NO!"

Stein's body is ripped apart inch by inch from the intensity of Corona Soul.

"LONG LIVE KOMBINAJO! The melting flames disintegrate his body to ashes and then vanish along with the massive ball of fire. Maerdym opens, cleaning up the remainders of Corona Soul and closing the story of Max Stein...

An aura of calmness sets upon the land. Light breaks through the dark atmosphere. Faces begin to smile, but many are wondering if it is really over.

"Doggie! Doggie!" Manny yells as he runs over to Darrel. "Doggie you did it!" He finally reaches Darrel giving him a hug.

"Ouch! Monkey not so hard. I'm pretty beat up."

"Oh. I'm sorry Doggie."

Darrel looks down on his little brother saying nothing, just emitting a grand smile on his face.

"Ha-ha I always believed in you Doggie."

"Thanks Monkey."

The others begin to rush over to Darrel.

"Darrel you beat him!" Karina shouts.

"Not bad Dustin," says Kyle.

"Excellent work my boy," Peng congratulates.

The people of New Rialto stampede to the others, giving thanks and shouting as loud as possible. Their celebration is well called for. Max Stein is gone. They can once again live in peace, but although the battle is over, the war has just begun. Maerdym light glows from the top of a small hill. At first the shine goes unnoticed but eventually catches everyone's eyes. The celebration dies down as the victors wait to see who or what will appear. A figure steps out of the Maerdym glow before it fades away.

Chapter 28: The Time has Come

"Good day everyone, you look exhausted."

From the Maerdym portal the time traveler Glen Heard has shown himself. All but one wonders who this stranger is. Glen's long hair sways in the wind, his presence is almost omniscience.

"Who is this guy?" Karina asked.

"Mr. Glen!" Manny shouts. To everyone's surprise the young boy is the only person who knows this being.

"We meet again Manny," Glen replies in a nonchalant way. "How have you been?"

"Ha-ha well it's only been like two days since I saw you."

Glen cuffs the back of his head in embarrassment. "Ah yes forgive me. Like I said last time, my time skips often leave me ignorant to what point in time the situation has reached. Hello Darrel, I would ask how you are doing but by the looks of things not too well."

Darrel is shocked by Glen's statement. "How do you know my name? And how do you know my brother?"

Peng looked at Manny. "Manny, is this who you met that night?"

"Yeah, this is Mr. Glen," Manny replied. "He can travel time."

"Travel time?!" Pepper asks in shock. "Then you must be a descendant of the great family of time!"

"Yes, I am Glen Heard, nice to meet you all. Excuse my hastiness but Manny, it's time."

Manny starred at Glen in agreement. He stood up as though ready for something to happen.

"Monkey, what is he talking about?" Darrel asked.

"I... I have to leave Doggie."

"Manny, what the hell are you talking about? Leave where? What's goin on?!"

"Manny, perhaps it's time you gave Darrel something," Glen spoke with a wink.

"Oh yeah right!" Manny turned to Darrel and kneeled down. He reached in his pocket for something while Darrel waited to see what his little brother could possibly have to justify leaving. Manny pulled out the pages from Truth given to him by Glen. Darrel hesitated to grab the papers.

"What's this?"

"Doggie, read the third paragraph on the top page."

Darrel reads not only the paragraph, but the entire page. "I don't get it. What does this mean?"

"Darrel," Glen announces. "The pages you hold in your hands are ripped directly from the prophecy."

"The prophecy?"

"Yes they come from my teacher's masterpiece. They come from Truth."

"WHAT!" Peng, Pepper, and many others shout out simultaneously.

"This cannot be!" Peng yells as he rushes over to see the pages himself. He gazes at them intensely. "This IS Truth!"

"Manny how did you get this?"

"Mr. Glen gave it to me. He said when the sun falls from the sky; I have to go with him."

"What? Manny you're not goin with anyone!"

"But Doggie-"

"-Manny wait," Glen interrupts. "Darrel I understand your feelings. Rest assure I will keep excellent care of your brother. We will return someday, but for now this is a journey Manny must take alone."

"Who the hell do you think you are?!" Darrel barks as he forces his body to stand.

"Darrel don't push yourself," says Peng. "You're still hurt."

"You think you can just come here and take my brother from me?! Fine, I'll fight you too!" Darrel's statement was bold especially seeing as how he was in no condition to stand, let alone fight.

"Doggie."

"No Manny. You're not goin with this guy!"

"Doggie, thank you."

"Thank me? For what?"

"For always protectin me. You are the best big brother I could ever have."

"Manny... No, please." Tears begin to fall from Darrel's eyes, though this time he doesn't try to hold them back. "Monkey, you can't leave. Monkey, your all I have left."

"No Doggie. Look around you, we have friends now! We're not alone anymore Doggie!"

Darrel looked away from Manny. He wiped the tears from his eyes and glanced at Peng who nodded in agreement. Darrel turned to Kyle. Kyle smiled back at Darrel's stare.

"He's right Darrel," said Pepper.

Finally Darrel looked over at Karina. She stared deeply into Darrel's eyes. Darrel couldn't help but see something familiar in this gaze, something comforting.

"I have to do this Doggie. It's what the Saver Piece wrote."

Darrel took a moment to gather himself. "It's like you're growing up right before my eyes Monkey. As much as I hate to admit it, you're not a little kid anymore. Monkey, I don't wanna lose you."

"You could never lose me Doggie. I'll always love you." Manny gives Darrel another big hug. The warmth of his love for his brother spread across the hearts of all who watched. The bond between brothers has never been as strong as these two. They both shed tears for each other.

Darrel turns his attention to Glen. "I will never forgive you if anything happens to him Glen."

"Understood. Manny, it's time we made our leave."

Manny and Darrel pried themselves from each other. Glen's soft hand suddenly appears on Manny's shoulder. They are then taken by the magnificent shine from Maerdym's light.

"Monkey! Monkey!"

"Doggie!"

The brothers reach out to each other hoping to touch one last time, but Manny's hands starts to fade and in an instant Manny and Glen are gone.

"Monkey... What have I done? How could I let you leave? Manny!"

Karina walks up to Darrel. She doesn't speak until they are face to face. They stare at each other like they are having a conversation with no words. Then she speaks.

"You did the right thing."

Darrel says nothing but continues to stare at Karina. Darrel is not only looking at her, but looking beyond her. He sees the same care his friends have for him as he cares for his brother.

"Thank you. This is all for him you know. I just want his dreams to come true."

"I think I finally get you. I know what you're dream is now. Your dream... is to make his dreams come true."

Darrel and Karina smile at each other while slipping into their own world. For a moment, they completely understand each other. The dust settles as the scene draws more and more calm. Outside of the falls a victory has been won, but inside the falls a life changing loss is set to happen.

Chapter 29: End of Saver

"Mom…"

"I'm leaving now Clark."

"Mom… I'm gonna miss you… so much."

"Cry for me Clark. I want to see your tears."

"I'm trying mom, I swear I am."

"Clark, whatever you do, don't let anything consume you. Always be what you believe is right. I have faith in you son, but you must have faith in yourself."

"I will mom. I promise."

"That's my baby. I'll be sure to tell your father you said hello."

Myra slips away. She is gone.

"MOM!" Clark shouts out to his mother in one final cry, without a tear in sight…

Throughout history Maerdym has connected the lives of every being with the will to dream. Like a spider's web, the bond is thin, but holds with incredibly durable strength. A mother's love is just as strong. So are a brother's love, and a grandfather's love. Those who are closest to us carve their names in our diamond hearts. For them one will do anything. When they are lost it presents a pain that seems unbearable. This pain can break us down, but it can also make us stronger. Our outcome depends solely on our dreams, and the path Maerdym takes us.

TO BE CONTINUED...

MAERDYM

BOOK TWO: OMNI

Darrel Dustin returns in the second chapter of the Maerdym saga, but this time he is without his little brother Manny. Though Darrel and his crew don't have much time to wait around for Manny's return because the Black Star is on the move! Darrel, Karina, and Peng must now face an opposition even more fierce than Max Stein. The Omni Piece has increased his dark control over the world and holds a power that seems unstoppable! Darrel and company must search their dreams and use the help of Truth to bring down a being born all powerful from the start!

But Paul and Erica will play their own part in this global battle. In book two find out the true connection between the siblings and their role in the evil Black Star organization.

Acknowledgements

Maerdym would never exist without the love and encouragement from everyone in my life.

I would like to personally thank my mother and father, Jacqueline Lusk Tucker and Rayford Tucker for everything they've done for me. Without them none of this would be possible. They don't know how much they mean to me and I am forever in their debt. To my little brother Daniel Tucker, you have been a great motivation to me. Of course I want to give thanks to all of my friends. You make me smile even when times are troubling.

And to a special someone, you'll always be in my heart, and in my dreams...

About the Author

DARNELL TUCKER was a high school senior when he began writing book one of the Maerdym series in between classes. Now a college student, he continues writing and is currently working on Maerdym book two: Omni at his home in Fort Worth, Texas.